MW00572224

THE
FULL MOON
COFFEE SHOP

THE
FULL MOON
COFFEE SHOP

A NOVEL

MAI MOCHIZUKI

TRANSLATED BY JESSE KIRKWOOD

BALLANTINE BOOKS

NEW YORK

Copyright © 2020 by Mai Mochizuki and Chihiro Sakurada

Translation copyright © 2024 by Jesse Kirkwood

Published in the United States by Ballantine Books, an imprint of Random House, a division of Penguin Random House LLC, New York.

This translation published in Great Britain in 2024 by Brazen, an imprint of Octopus Publishing Group Ltd, London.

Originally published in Japan as *Mangetsu Kohiten no Hoshiyomi* by Bungeishunju Ltd. in 2020.

Illustrations by Chihiro Sakurada

Hardback ISBN 9780593726822
International edition ISBN 9780593973783
Ebook ISBN 9780593726839

Printed in the United States of America on acid-free paper

randomhousebooks.com

2   4   6   8   9   7   5   3   1

First U.S. Edition

Book design by Sara Bereta

CONTENTS

THE
FULL MOON
COFFEE SHOP

"The Full Moon Coffee Shop has no fixed location.

"It might appear in the middle of a familiar shopping arcade, by the station at the end of the railway line, or on a quiet riverbank.

"At the Full Moon Coffee Shop, we don't take your order; instead we bring you desserts, meals, and drinks—selected just for you.

"Who knows—maybe it's all a dream."

With these words, the large tortoiseshell cat that had appeared in front of me narrowed his eyes and smiled.

PROLOGUE

It was early April and my apartment windows were wide open. A crisp spring breeze swept in—along with the beautiful sound of Elgar's *Salut d'Amour* (*Love's Greeting*) being played on the piano.

As if summoned by the music, a cat appeared on the railing of my balcony. Perhaps it belonged to one of the other residents. After all, pets *were* allowed in my apartment block. It was a regular tortoiseshell cat, its fur a pretty mix of brown and black. In spite of the obvious danger, it picked its way along the railing with a dainty assurance. I found myself gazing at it in total admiration. Maybe it was the clear blue sky or the pink cherry blossom trees in the distance, but the whole scene resembled a painting.

Meanwhile, I was cooking lunch—or pretending to. In reality, I was just chopping up some spring onion to chuck on top of my instant ramen. Sure, I was going to add some chopped carrots, bean sprouts, and spinach stir-fried in sesame oil, but it wasn't exactly refined cuisine. And the result definitely didn't look like *any* kind of painting.

The cat had come to a halt halfway along the railing and was narrowing its eyes in rapture, as if it, too, was appreciating the music coming from the piano below. Its long tail swished back and forth like a pendulum.

I lived in a tiny studio apartment, and the kitchen was only a few steps from the balcony. The cat noticed me and looked around, giving me a little *meow*.

Salut de chat, I thought, smiling to myself. I washed my hands and made my way over to the balcony, but by the time I slid the screen door open with a clatter, the cat had disappeared.

I glanced around, but it was nowhere to be seen. I lived on the third floor. Worrying it might have slipped, I looked over the edge of the railing, but there was no sign of it down there, either. A cat would never fall like that, I reminded myself. Relieved, I leaned against the railing. *Salut d'Amour* came to an end and now began Chopin's Étude, op. 10, no. 3, sometimes known as the "Farewell."

I sighed, drooping my head slightly. Farewells were not what I wanted to be thinking about. I knew that breaking up was always hard, but it felt even harder when you were a forty-year-old woman who thought she'd finally found "the one." We'd been together so long that I'd begun to assume we always would be.

But I realize you can't take anything for granted. I mean, after all, even cats sometimes lose their footing. This thought made me anxious, and I looked back down at the ground. There was still no sign of the cat. Wherever it had gone, it seemed to be doing just fine.

If anyone had taken a fall, it was me.

Where had I gone so wrong?

Hearing excited voices from below, I glanced down once more and saw a group of children strolling down the street. They looked to be in the early years of primary school, and would be on their spring holidays now. A wave of nostalgia rushed over me, and I wondered how my old pupils were doing. *Maybe*, I thought, *I shouldn't have quit teaching after all.*

But if I was still a teacher, in my present state, some little tyrant would inevitably run up to me and ask the merciless question, "Miss, why aren't you married?" It would have been enough to make me burst into tears in front of the entire class.

Yes, I was glad I'd given that job up. Nodding emphatically as if to convince myself, I pulled the screen door closed and made my way back inside.

Before I knew it, the piano playing had come to an end.

CHAPTER 1

AQUARIUS TRIFLE

水瓶座のトライフル

MIZUKI SERIKAWA

1

Delicious.

Even if I did say so myself. Instant ramen topped with vegetables and spring onion: not the most elegant meal, but one that never failed to hit the spot.

I took my empty bowl to the kitchen, gave it a quick rinse, and set it on the dish rack. Then I took a cloth and gave the dining table a thorough wipe. It was barely big enough for one person to eat at. In my tiny apartment, this was where I ate and worked.

I poured myself a coffee, positioned my laptop back on the table, and sat down. Then, taking a sip from my mug, I began flicking through my reference materials.

I was looking at a character sheet, its pages packed with illustrations of a handsome young man.

What's this guy's story again...?

He was supposed to be the son of a rich and distinguished family, but his hair was a mix of red, blue, and yellow, and he didn't look very distinguished to me. But then again, we were talking about a video game here. People didn't care too much about the details.

I wrote scripts for a living. Right now, I was working on one for a mobile dating game. Not the main script—someone else was doing that. *My* job was to write the script for when the player ended up with a supporting character rather than the "happy ending" where they managed to win the heart of the hero. It was a middle-of-the-road sort of ending, which meant the script had to be pretty middling, too. The idea was that the player would feel vaguely dissatisfied by the outcome, but would also keep playing the game.

It wasn't a very long script, either. A thirty-kilobyte episode. It must be only video-game writers who have their work measured not in pages or words, but in kilobytes. I checked my instructions.

End with a scene where he kisses her on the cheek or forehead. Location should be near a body of water.

Right. No kissing on the lips. As for the body of water . . . the male character was supposed to be the indoor type, so a seaside or river didn't quite feel right. A hotel pool would do the trick.

I leafed through the pages, then opened up my notepad. The writing inside was such a squiggly mess that anyone else would struggle to decipher it. It outlined my plot—if you could call it that—for the character.

When writing the side character, the goal was always to make the player feel slightly frustrated, so they'd think to themselves: *I don't like how that turned out—guess I'll have to try dating the hero if I want my happy ending!*

That meant including a lot of failed dates, and any love scenes had to be pretty subdued affairs. In its own way, it was pretty challenging work.

When I'd finished reviewing my notes, I started to write. Soon the sound of my fingers tapping away at my computer keyboard fell into step with the music I was playing.

Most of the game scripts I worked on were pretty conventional. I was good at writing stories like that, so I enjoyed the work. Of course, I'd have preferred to write the love scenes for the hero.

But that was more than I could ask for at that point—even if it was true I'd once worked on much more important things. I tried to clear my head and get back to writing.

Thirty kilobytes could be various page lengths, depending on the amount of text, but it was basically the length of a short story. When I was about a third of the way through, I sat up in my chair and straightened my back. The clock showed three in the afternoon.

I've only been working for two hours?

So that was how long I could focus for these days—

two whole hours. The Mizuki of a decade ago would have just been getting started. . . . Just then, my phone vibrated on the table.

> Mizuki, it's been a long time! This is Akari Nakayama. Sorry to be so last-minute, but I'm in the Kansai area on business. In fact, I'm in Kyoto right now. Do you have time to meet?

The sight of the sender's name was enough to set my heart racing. Akari worked at the TV production company I used to write for. She was a director these days. A month ago, I'd plucked up all my courage and sent her a TV pitch. She seemed to be in Kyoto on other business, but the fact that she'd even bothered to get in touch had to mean she wanted to talk about it.

I wrote back:

> Of course! Would love to meet up.

Her reply came soon after.

> **Wonderful. How about the lobby of that hotel where we used to have our meetings? Can you be there in an hour?**

I replied:

> **No problem.**

I immediately closed my computer and opened the door to the tiny storage room I was using as a closet. Not knowing what to wear, I ended up plumping for the safety of a suit.

I stood in front of the washbasin. There was no room for a dresser in my apartment, so my makeup kit lived by the basin. I got out my foundation and started dabbing it onto my skin.

Urgh, why does it look so weird?

I hadn't been out much recently, except to the nearby supermarket, and I wasn't going to put on makeup for that; I just wore a face mask instead. My skin, surprised by this abrupt reacquaintance with the world of cosmetics, seemed to have decided it was having none of it. I used to put a lot of effort into this kind of thing. In fact, the old me would have laughed if she could see me now.

Still, no use complaining. I carried on applying my makeup, painting my eyebrows, and putting on lipstick, then threw on a light cardigan, grabbed my bag, and headed out. Leaving the apartment block, I made my way toward the station. Technically, I lived in Kyoto. But my neighborhood was a far cry from the beautiful, old-world image most people had of the city. In fact, it was no different from your average residential area.

I boarded my train and settled into my seat with a sigh of relief.

Another message from Akari:

> The lobby was busy, so I've moved to the ground-floor café. I'm just getting some work done, so there's no rush.

I could just picture her in the hotel café with her laptop open. Like a lot of people in the TV industry, she could work anywhere. I used to be like that— scribbling away in cafés and all sorts of places. Recently, though, I'd been staying at home unless I had some reason to go out. Why waste money on a cup of coffee? It was the same with food. I mainly ate instant meals, sometimes adding vegetables in a vague attempt to be healthy. That was probably the reason why my skin was looking so bad . . .

I looked down at my phone and checked the ratings and reviews for my last drama, which was currently airing. I felt a pang in my chest, and quickly averted my eyes from my phone.

There were some more kids on the train, perhaps on their way home from primary school. Year two or three, by the looks of it. Instead of the usual firm-sided school backpacks, they were sporting chic brown leather bags—a sign they went to a private school. They were riding the train to school all by themselves. *Good for them*, I thought.

"Excuse me," came a low voice from my side. "Are you . . . Miss Serikawa?"

My heart skipped a beat. I stared in bewilderment at the woman sitting next to me. She looked as if she were in her midtwenties, though she had such a calm presence that I wondered if she might be a little older.

Even a quick glance told me she was fashionable; her short but carefully manicured nails and her lightly colored hair all made me think she might work in the beauty industry. Maybe she used to be my stylist?

"Sorry, I hope I didn't startle you. I was actually one of your pupils at primary school . . ."

Ah, I thought, the tension dissipating from my shoulders. An old pupil. That made sense.

"You were a really great teacher, you know."

I gave an embarrassed shrug in response.

Back then I'd been no more than a substitute. I only really came into contact with the pupils when one of the main teachers was on leave. It was great that this woman thought I had been a good teacher, but I didn't remember us ever spending enough time together to warrant that sort of praise.

"You used to accompany us home after school," she added, seeming to notice my confusion.

It was true that I'd often walked the kids home. Their main teacher was always busy preparing classes, so the job naturally fell to the substitute. Still, it wasn't always plain sailing. You never knew what the younger kids would do next, so you had to really keep your eye on them. Sometimes just getting them to line up and walk in a straight line was a challenge. As they walked, I'd try to come up with all sorts of ways to stop them from getting bored—starting a game of word association or engaging them in conversation.

"Brings back memories," I said, smiling at her with a rush of nostalgia.

We carried on talking. It turned out I'd guessed right: my old pupil was a hairdresser these days. When we got to her stop, she apologized again for startling me, bowed, and hopped off the train.

I should have at least asked for her name, I thought to myself, bowing back as she walked off. As I settled back into my seat, a warm feeling spread through my body. Becoming a primary-school teacher had been something I'd always dreamed of. The job came with its challenges, but at times like this I was so glad I'd done it.

So why did I switch to scriptwriting?

At first, I'd done both jobs at the same time. Substitute teachers were allowed to take on other employment, so I'd done scriptwriting on the side.

But when I was finally given the chance to become a full-time teacher, I had to choose which road to go down. I decided to give up my career in teaching to become a full-time scriptwriter.

How many years had it been since then? Enough for my former pupils to be adults with jobs by now—and for me to have entered my forties.

These days I lived in the grip of an anxiety that seemed as if it would never end. If I'd stuck with teaching, no matter how tough it might have felt occasionally, my life would have been a lot more stable. And my fears about my future wouldn't have kept me up at night, either.

I bit my lip and looked down squarely at my lap.

2

From the station, I made my way across the Sanjo Bridge and toward the hotel where I was meeting Akari. It had been a while since I'd been into central Kyoto.

Until two years ago, I thought with a sigh, I'd actually lived here, in an airy, spacious apartment overlooking the wide Kamo River, with a separate living room and bedroom. In the mornings, I'd take walks along the river or sip tea on my wide balcony. Back then, I used to hang out in a café on Kiyamachi Street, overlooking the Takase—a smaller waterway that ran parallel to the Kamo. I loved that place. I wondered what had become of it now.

Lost in my thoughts, I headed north from Sanjo Street, then west along Oike Street. The hotel was just alongside the town hall. I'd had plenty of work meetings here in the past. Feeling my pulse quicken, I made my way into the lobby and from there through to the café.

The place was pretty full, with plenty of foreign tourists dotted around the room. But looking over at the seats by the window, I managed to spot Akari Nakayama.

Production-company staff tended to dress pretty casually, but I'd never seen Akari in anything other than a snappy suit that reflected her dedication to the job. Today was no exception: there she was in a black pantsuit. I'd expected to find her tapping away at a laptop, but it was actually a tablet I spotted in her hands.

"Akari! Sorry to keep you waiting," I said, walking over to her. She looked up and jumped to her feet.

"Ah, Mizuki! Sorry to call on you like this all of a sudden. Thanks for making time."

"It's no trouble at all, really."

"You live just around here, don't you?"

I gave a vague laugh and shook my head. "I've moved, actually."

"Oh, now I really *am* sorry. I only suggested this place because I thought you were nearby!"

I reassured her that it was no big deal, and we took our seats. The coffee I ordered arrived quickly.

"Did you just get into town?"

"Yeah. I'm meeting someone from the local network this evening."

"That reminds me, how's our old director doing?"

"Oh, she's a producer now."

"Moving up in the world! And you're a director these days, aren't you?"

"Must be weird for you, I guess. You knew me back when I was a newbie!"

Ever since Akari had joined the company, she'd been a real go-getter, holding herself and everyone else to the highest standards. I always knew she was destined for great things. In fact, that was why I'd decided to send her an email the previous month—that no-nonsense attitude of hers was exactly what I needed. I don't think I'd have felt comfortable reaching out to anyone else.

I cleared my throat slightly. With us idly chatting away like this, it was getting harder and harder to broach the subject that was at the forefront of my mind: the pitch I'd sent her.

So, what did you think of the pitch?

The words were on the tip of my tongue, but I couldn't quite bring myself to spit them out. There was something else I needed to get off my chest first.

"Akari," I said, my head drooping. "I'm really sorry for all the trouble I put you through."

She shook her head.

"Don't worry, Mizuki, I get how rough it was for you. You were always way more perceptive than most people, and it really showed in your work. But when people started becoming critical, I guess that just made things even more painful for you."

Akari took a sip of her coffee.

I remained silent and bowed my head again.

"You really did write some excellent shows, Mizuki."

She said this while squinting at me as though she was looking at something dazzling.

She was using the past tense, of course.

•   •   •

I'd debuted as a scriptwriter at twenty, when I was still a student, after winning the Best Drama Screenplay award in a competition organized by a major television network. After that, I'd started writing scripts regularly, though it never paid enough to make ends meet.

After graduating from university, I went ahead and became a substitute primary-school teacher. The scriptwriting work felt like a side hustle, a hangover from my student days.

But then one of the scripts I'd written at university ended up becoming a huge hit. It was a late-night drama starring a bunch of complete unknowns, which led to even greater accolades for my work.

After that success, bigger jobs started coming my way. Still in my twenties, I was quickly dubbed a "hitmaker" and given the task of penning a prime-time drama script. With all this going on, it wasn't long before I devoted myself entirely to scriptwriting.

But then, in my midthirties, everything changed. All of a sudden, it was as though my previous successes counted for absolutely nothing. The ratings for my shows plummeted.

The final blow came when I was asked to write the script for a drama starring an insanely talented cast, which everyone assumed was going to be a huge success. It aired during prime time, and yet the ratings never made it past single figures. It was as though I'd committed a war crime.

Still, even after that, they were willing to give me a chance—after all, flops happened from time to time. Surely whatever I turned out next would draw in viewers? But then the next drama tanked, and so did the one after that. The backlash against me grew and grew. Pretty soon, I was working with the new kids on the block, like Akari, instead of the veteran directors.

At that point, everything fell apart. The constant criticism and stress got to me so much that I stopped showing up at work. I disappeared completely, ignoring every call or text that came my way. Meanwhile, Akari had to pick up the slack, which must have been a nightmare. And yet she was the only one who kept trying to get in touch, when everyone else had written me off.

Eventually even she stopped calling, and I found myself completely unemployed. I was burning through all the cash I'd saved up during my days as a "hitmaker," and soon it became hard to maintain my old life. I decided to trade my chic apartment for something more budget-friendly, which was how I ended up in my current place. And I decided to sell off all the fancy furniture I'd accumulated over the years of success.

After a while, I started working on scripts again, but under the pen name "Serika." I answered an advertisement I saw online for a mobile-game script-writer, managed to get the job, and had been scraping a living ever since.

Since the work was under a pseudonym, I had nothing to show for it afterward, and it wasn't as if it was going to lead to anything more promising. But putting my real name to anything at this point just felt too terrifying.

* * *

"Seriously, I love your work, Mizuki. You know, *Path to the Summit, Classroom of Light* . . . The way the protagonist starts at the bottom and slowly works their way up to the top—it's pure magic. That never-say-die spirit is *so* inspiring . . ."

I turned away, self-conscious in the face of this praise. For all their various plots and settings, all my scripts had one thing in common. They were the story of the underdog who persevered against the odds and ended up getting their just reward. In other words, a classic success story.

"Which is why I was really excited to read the pitch you sent."

My pulse started racing. I could feel my hands shaking with a mixture of excitement and anxiety. I looked up at her.

"I'm sorry, Mizuki—they turned it down. I took it to the meeting, but the execs just weren't convinced." She cast her eyes down apologetically.

"Oh, don't worry," I said hurriedly, shaking my head and smiling. "I'm flattered you even presented it to them."

Akari was dedicated enough to her job that I'd dared to hope she'd at least look at my proposal. I'd never expected her to actually pitch it to the network executives. I was more than happy; I was shocked. At the same time, this confirmation that I just wasn't cut out for the industry anymore felt like a blow to the chest.

"I guess that's that, then. Thank you anyway, Akari," I said, smiling, as I bowed to her. Inside, though, I was still reeling.

For a brief moment, she squinted at me fondly.

"I'm sorry I couldn't do more to help," she said, quickly bowing in return. I shook my head and told her she didn't need to apologize.

"I hate to dash off," she continued, "but I have my meeting soon . . ."

"Oh, of course. Sorry to keep you."

"See you around!" she said, and walked out of the café.

•　　•　　•

After Akari left, I sat gazing vacantly out of the window.

Eventually, I found myself wondering why on earth she had summoned me to the café just to shoot me down.

But then, as she'd said, she'd thought I was still living around here. And she'd gone to the trouble of telling me in person, when she could just have done it by email. Maybe I should be grateful instead?

Was it time to give up?

Maybe this rejection was a sign. I needed to stop clinging to my past accomplishments and leave the world of scriptwriting for good. That seemed to be the message . . .

I brought my coffee, now cold, to my mouth.

"Hey, I couldn't help overhearing your conversation," came a voice from the neighboring table. "So you're Mizuki Serikawa, the scriptwriter?"

I looked up abruptly. The person addressing me so casually turned out to be a slim young man, maybe around twenty years old.

He looked pretty flash; in fact, his appearance bordered on the absurd. His hair was dyed blond on the outside and light blue on the inside, and he must have been wearing colored contacts because his eyes were a beautiful green. He was also sporting a pair of red-rimmed glasses—perhaps an attempt to offset the color of his eyes.

Phone in hand, he studied me for a moment, then broke into a sudden grin. He had an impressive set of canines.

"Erm . . . yes?" I nodded awkwardly, wondering why someone this young knew who I was.

"I have to say, I love your shows," he said, squinting at me admiringly from behind his glasses. There was that casual tone again. Still, praise was praise.

"But," he continued, "let's be honest. They've sort of lost their appeal these days, haven't they?"

I started in my seat.

"*Sorry?*"

I was so taken aback I didn't know what else to say.

"Times have changed. If you don't change with them, you're guaranteed to flop. You see it all the time, especially in your industry. I mean, these shows are broadcast to the masses! If you're working in TV, you *have* to stay current. Otherwise," he continued, holding up an index finger as he rattled on, "you're a goner, no matter what kind of a genius you are."

I could hear him just fine, but somehow his words weren't registering properly. What was this kid trying to say? That, as a scriptwriter, I'd passed my sell-by date—that I should know my place?

I did not need *him* to tell *me* that.

Just as I could feel tears welling in my eyes, an older man appeared and boxed him around the ears from behind.

"Ouch!"

"What's wrong with you? Where are your manners?" The man issuing this reprimand must have been around forty, and wore a black suit and gray tie. His jet-black hair, cool gaze, and well-defined features were altogether striking. He sat down opposite the youngster.

His dad, maybe?

But they seemed too close in age for that. And they looked nothing alike. In contrast to the eccentric-looking kid, the guy in the suit had the stern composure of a professor.

"Sorry about him," he said, bowing politely.

"That's okay," I said, shaking my head.

"Mizuki, this guy's a fan of yours," said the kid with a giggle. The man in the suit glanced sharply at him, then turned to me and gave another quick bow.

"Again, I really do apologize."

I shook my head again.

Uncle and nephew, maybe?

"I'm happy to hear you're a fan."

To be honest, I found it almost suspicious that someone would still think of me that way.

"Your works depict protagonists brimming with good old common sense, striving to do their best in the face of myriad challenges. I really can't help but admire them."

His tone and expression were deadly serious. I

31

could feel myself blushing. He seemed to really mean what he said—that he liked my work.

"But the way they're written—it's just so out of touch, isn't it?" said the kid, joining his hands together behind his head. Then, noticing the man glaring at him, he shrugged and said, "Okay, okay, I'm sorry!"

"Right, you, let's get going," said the man, getting to his feet.

"Sure thing!" said the kid, jumping up. "Oh, Mizuki, if you *do* want to catch up with the times, you should check this place out. It's a full moon to-night, so they'll be open." He placed a business card in front of me.

On it were the words: *The Full Moon Coffee Shop.*

Below was an address. *South of the Nijo-Kiyamachi intersection*, it said, with typical Kyoto vagueness. That wasn't far from this hotel.

"I don't remember any cafés like that around here . . ." I murmured. But when I looked up, the pair had vanished. I scanned the room for them, but they were nowhere to be seen.

I looked out of the window. It was already getting dark.

Catching up with the times, huh?

Presumably it was a coffee shop, as the name suggested.

Would they be able to teach me something there? I wondered. *Would they charge extra for that, on top of my drink? What if it was super expensive?*

The kid's face flitted across my mind. There was something suspicious about that flashy appearance of his. Not to mention his weirdly casual vibe.

I decided I should head home. Even if it really was just a coffee shop, I couldn't spare the cash.

I slowly got to my feet and made my way out.

3

It wasn't far from the hotel to the nearest metro station or bus stop, but I didn't feel like heading home straightaway. Instead, I wandered in the direction of Kiyamachi Street.

This was the heart of Kyoto. There were plenty of people around, but for a spring holiday evening, the area was surprisingly quiet.

As I reached Kiyamachi Street, I came to a halt. If I continued north, I'd presumably find the coffee shop that the kid had mentioned.

Might as well see what the place looks like from outside.

I gave in to this inner voice and headed up the street. On my right was a row of old townhouses, while on my left the Takase River murmured along.

A bridge with the word *Ichi-no-funairi* engraved on it came into view.

A boat laden with sake casks was bobbing on the canal. About four hundred years ago, a wealthy merchant had built a canal between Nijo and Fushimi, complete with nine docking places for loading and unloading goods. This had been one of them, and the name engraved on the bridge meant "first docking place." The boat I could see was a reproduction of a vessel from those days. Cherry-blossom petals were falling around it. It was quite the atmospheric scene.

Kyoto really is pretty special, I thought.

I was from Hiroshima, and I'd first come here on a trip with my primary school. I'd fallen in love with the city, and begged my parents to let me attend university there. Back then, everything seemed to fall into my lap.

These days, though, all that seemed like a dream from the distant past. . . .

It was then that I noticed the sign.

THE FULL MOON COFFEE SHOP

There it was: the café's name, together with an arrow. I gulped at the sight.

So it really does exist . . .

The arrow pointed down a long, narrow alleyway. Candles were dotted at intervals along the ground. It was a truly dreamlike sight.

What exactly *was* this place? My curiosity was beginning to overpower me.

I'd always been the inquisitive sort. When writing my scripts, I spent as much time out and about researching them as I did writing them. Somehow,

35

I'd forgotten how thrilling an adventure like this could be.

Nervously, I made my way down the alley until I came to a tunnel-like entrance, which I ducked through to find myself on the banks of the wide Kamo River.

I looked up to see the full moon. Its rays were glinting off the cherry blossom trees. The river was a torrent, glittering in the moonlight.

Looking downstream, I could make out what appeared to be an isolated train carriage, positioned below the perfectly circular moon. Squinting, I realized that it was more like a small bus or truck. It had two windows, each with a small counter in front of it that would be just big enough for one person to eat at. From the truck hung a light designed to look like a full moon, and at the front was a sign that said: THE FULL MOON COFFEE SHOP.

With a name like that, I'd been expecting something quaint and old-fashioned, but this looked more like a trendy pop-up café. Its soft lights glowed against the dark backdrop of the riverbank.

As far as I could see, there was no indoor seating,

just three sets of tables and chairs that had been set out in front of the truck.

On one of the chairs was a stuffed rabbit. Did that mean it was reserved? A coffee cup had even been positioned in front of the rabbit. A lantern flickered on the table.

"Hello there!" came a man's voice from inside the truck. "Please, sit wherever you like." The voice was gentle and calm, but I couldn't see anyone.

I bowed, though it didn't seem as if whoever had spoken could see me, then took a seat at one of the empty tables.

I'd had no idea there was a charming café like this on the bank of the Kamo. That kid had said something about them being open because it was a full moon, so presumably it was only here temporarily. I was glad I'd tried my luck.

For a moment I simply sat there, resting my chin in my hands. Then I looked up—and gasped.

The sky was teeming with stars. It was the kind of dazzling night sky you never see in Japan anymore, with the Milky Way swirling vividly across the dark expanse. It was like being at a planetarium.

"Amazing," I murmured in awe.

"The coffee here *is* good, isn't it?" came a voice from the table just behind me. I twisted around in surprise.

The voice had come from the chair in which, a moment ago, a stuffed rabbit had been sitting. Now, though, it was occupied by an elderly gentleman. He was dressed in a black tailcoat, as if he was on the way to some fancy dinner party.

When did he get here?

He finished his coffee, savoring every last drop, then slowly got to his feet and returned his cup to the truck.

"Thank you for that! Outstanding coffee, as usual."

"Thank you, sir."

What with the elderly gentleman standing in the way, and the bright lights shining from the café, I still couldn't quite see the man who seemed to run the place.

The older gentleman strolled smartly off, stopping for a moment to flash a smile in my direction. I bowed back at him. As he passed, he seemed to murmur something to me.

I looked up, meaning to ask what he'd said, but what I saw left me speechless. The gentleman had turned into a . . . rabbit. There he went, walking on two legs as he made his way along the riverbank.

What on earth . . .

I rubbed my eyes and looked again. The rabbit had vanished.

Am I imagining things?

As I stared in bewilderment, I heard that gentle voice again.

"Sorry for the wait."

I turned around—and now found myself facing a huge tortoiseshell cat. It was proffering a tray in my direction.

"What the . . ." My mouth gaped as I looked up at the cat.

The creature must have been more than six feet tall. It was standing on its hind legs and wearing a navy-blue apron. Its face was perfectly round, its smiling eyes like crescent moons.

The cat was talking.

The cat was holding a tray.

Most of all, the cat was . . . enormous.

39

Could it be someone in an incredibly lifelike animal suit? I could feel myself go goggle-eyed as I tried to make sense of the scene.

The cat was very fluffy, and I found myself briefly thinking how soothing he'd be to hug. My mouth simply opened and closed silently, like a goldfish gulping for air. No words would come.

The cat smiled. He seemed thoroughly entertained by my bewilderment. "Thank you very much for dropping by. Sorry if this is all a bit of a shock!"

I shook my head slightly, trying vaguely to reassure him.

"It's very nice to meet you," he said, setting a glass down on the table. "Welcome to the Full Moon Coffee Shop."

I murmured a thank you, and gazed down at the glass. It was small, slightly curved, and contained three ice cubes and some water. At the gentle impact of the glass being set down on the table, tiny shards of light began to shimmer on the surface of the water, like gold dust. Baffled, I leaned in to get a closer look, but the golden specks had disappeared.

I took a long gulp of the water to steady my nerves.

It tasted purer than any water I'd ever drunk. As it trickled down my throat, it seemed to dissolve directly into me, spreading around my entire body.

The ice clinked around in the glass. This being a spring evening, there was still a chill in the air. And yet somehow I now felt very warm.

The iced water seemed to have calmed me down slightly.

"I run this place, by the way. Sorry my waiter was so rude earlier."

I cocked my head to one side.

"Your . . . waiter?"

"That's right. I believe he told you about this place?"

At this point, two other cats appeared and hopped onto the table. These two, at least, were a normal size. One of them was vaguely exotic-looking, with big ears and a slim body. I knew my cat breeds: this was a Singapura. The other one was a black and white tuxedo cat. The Singapura's big, round eyes were a beautiful green, while the tuxedo's were gray, narrow, and turned slightly upward at the corners.

"Ah, Mizuki. You came!" said the Singapura.

I'd already seen a giant cat talking, so an ordinary one doing the same was slightly less impressive—but still astonishing.

"What . . . ?"

The tuxedo cat seemed to consider me for a moment, then bowed.

"Miss Serikawa. I *am* sorry about earlier."

The two of them bore a very close resemblance to the boy and the man I'd met at the café.

"Are you . . . the people I met earlier?" I couldn't have opened my eyes any wider. "What are you— demons or something?"

The three cats looked at one another, then burst out laughing.

"We do turn into humans from time to time, but we're certainly not demons," said the tuxedo cat.

"Yeah. Jeez. Bit rude!" said the Singapura. I felt my expression stiffening.

"I'm sorry," I said hastily. "So, is this place . . . for cats?" I asked with a gulp.

A café for cats.

I was living in some absurd fairy tale. Maybe I'd fallen asleep? I mean, this kind of thing only happened in dreams. Yes, this had to be a dream. Once I had convinced myself of that, I began to relax slightly.

In response to my question, the three cats exchanged a series of glances, then nodded vaguely.

"You could say so, yes," said the tuxedo cat.

"Though this isn't our real form, either . . ." said the Singapura, scratching behind his ear. Just as he was about to go on, the tuxedo cat cleared his throat loudly. The Singapura hastily clapped a paw to his mouth.

"The Full Moon Coffee Shop has no fixed location," said the master of the café. "It might appear in the middle of a familiar shopping street, by the station at the end of the railway line, or on a quiet riverbank. And at this café, we don't ask for your order." He put a paw to his chest and bowed ceremoniously.

"You mean I don't get to choose from a menu?"

"That's right," the tortoiseshell said with a nod.

"That elderly gentleman just now was drinking a coffee. Are you saying he didn't order it?"

"Exactly."

"It's just . . . I was thinking I'd order one myself."

The master smiled apologetically.

43

"We usually serve coffee to people who've been through all the highs and lows of life—who've experienced both the bitter and the sweet. Not to someone as young as yourself, I'm afraid." The master chuckled.

"Young? I'm forty."

"In astrological terms, you're still in your Mars phase. That's young, all right."

"Oh." I sighed in confusion. "Mars phase?"

"You're familiar with the planets in our solar system, I assume? Other than this one, I mean."

"Well, yes, of course." I nodded. What was the mnemonic we'd used at school? *Sui-kin-chika-moku-do-ten-kai-mei*... "Mercury, Venus, Mars, Jupiter, Saturn, Uranus, Neptune, and Pluto ... right?"

"Indeed," said the master, holding up what seemed to be his equivalent of an index finger. "Actually, when it comes to life phases, we also include the Sun and the Moon, in the following order: Moon, Mercury, Venus, Sun, Mars, Jupiter, Saturn, Uranus, Neptune, and Pluto."

I listened as the master launched into a full explanation of the "life phases."

"First comes the Moon phase, from birth to the

age of seven. It's when you develop your perception, sensitivity, and emotions.

"Next is the Mercury phase. Age eight to fifteen. Your world is still a small one, but you gradually emerge into society and soak up all sorts of knowledge. Among humans, this corresponds to the early years of school.

"Then you have the Venus phase. Sixteen to twenty-five. It's when you start taking an interest in your appearance, discover what it really means to have fun and learn to love. The Venus phase is associated with leisure, pleasure, and romance." *That makes sense,* I thought, *seeing as it coincides with the last years of high school and college.*

"After that is the Sun phase—from twenty-six to thirty-five. Building on what you learned during Mercury, and the fun you had during Venus, you finally learn what it means to make your own way in life.

"And right now you're in your Mars phase, which is from thirty-six to forty-five. It's when you take ownership of everything you've learned and let your true ability shine."

"People do say your forties are the prime of your working life, don't they?" I murmured hesitantly.

The master went on to explain that the Jupiter phase was from forty-six to fifty-five, Saturn from fifty-six to seventy, Uranus from seventy-one to eighty-four, and Neptune from eighty-five until you died. The Pluto phase, meanwhile, referred to the moment of your death.

"And so, in astrological terms, your Mars phase is when you finally begin stepping into 'adulthood.' Making you, my friend, still very much a young woman!"

I felt myself blushing at his use of "young woman."

"But," continued the master, "sometimes, if you haven't properly completed your Moon, Mercury, Venus, and Sun phases, it can be hard to progress to the next one."

"Properly completed? What does that mean?" I asked, leaning forward.

The master smiled and waved a hand, as if now was not the time. "A more important question is: Are you hungry?"

As soon as he asked, it dawned on me that I was famished. Now that I thought about it, I hadn't eaten anything since those instant noodles I had for lunch. This dream was proving strangely realistic.

A faint, sweet smell wafted over. I looked up and saw the master approaching with a tray laden with pancakes.

"These are one of our specialties," said the tortoiseshell cat proudly. "Full Moon Pancakes." He set them down on the table, together with a cup of black tea. Multiple pancakes were stacked on a round white plate, and on top of them was a sphere of butter.

"A very popular dish on full-moon nights," said the Singapura.

"Please enjoy them with a generous drizzle of Astral Syrup," added the tuxedo cat.

I nodded and poured the syrup over the butter. As the name suggested, the Astral Syrup gave off a star-like, golden shimmer. It trickled slowly onto the butter, then oozed onto the pancakes.

I bowed a little awkwardly and reached for the knife and fork. The cutlery had been polished to a

47

mirrorlike shine. I cut myself a bite-sized piece and placed the morsel in my mouth. A delicate, gentle sweetness enveloped my taste buds. The combination of the rich butter with the Astral Syrup was quite extraordinary. It tasted somehow nostalgic, but equally like nothing I'd ever eaten.

That was *exactly* what I needed.

It was as though I'd never eaten pancakes before. In fact, this was probably how I felt when I ate them for the first time.

Next, I reached for the cup of tea. No milk or sugar—just straight black tea. I took a sip. It had all the rich flavor of black tea without the slightest bitterness. I felt its warmth filling my throat and radiating gently throughout my entire body.

"This is delicious, too," I said, setting the cup down.

"The tea leaves were picked on the night of a full moon. They have liberating qualities," explained the master.

"Liberating qualities?"

"Yes. The full moon gives us the power to let things go. That includes negative emotions such as regret, jealousy, or obsession."

Regret. Jealousy. Obsession.

I took another sip of the tea. Those weren't the only things I wanted to let go of. There was also my fear of what others thought of me. My terror of being criticized. My habit of not facing up to the truth.

"I think I could do with a bit of letting go," I murmured. Tears had begun to trickle down my cheeks. I hastily wiped them away.

"Oh, don't worry—let it all out. There's no one here but us cats, is there?" said the tuxedo breezily.

The master looked down at me with his kind eyes. "Never really had a good cry before, have you? You know, when things feel tough, or frustrating, crying can do you a world of good. Water washes everything away."

I'd been through so much recently, and yet I'd never let myself cry. All I'd ever done was curl up in a terrified ball, trying to hide from the world.

The tears running down my cheeks were incredibly warm. When they dripped from my chin, they seemed to shimmer slightly, just like the Astral Syrup. I gulped as more of them welled in my eyes. All the pain I'd been suppressing seemed to be pouring out of me.

I cried for what felt like a long time. When I looked up, the master had disappeared. So had the Singapura and the tuxedo cat.

Then I turned and saw them, waiting inside the Full Moon Coffee Shop.

Please, take your time, I seemed to hear them say.

I bowed back at them, then looked down at the table. My pancakes were still warm, and by now the butter had melted and was sinking into their fluffy surface.

I picked my cutlery back up and started eating again. Somewhere I could hear the gentle tinkle of a piano. Beethoven's Piano Sonata No. 8 in C minor. The *Pathétique.*

The name had always sounded a little sad to me, but there was something undeniably soothing about the piece. The lilting tempo seemed to conjure up a meandering walk along a riverbank just like this one—pausing to gaze up at the moon or the cherry blossoms, losing yourself in memories of the past.

All sorts of things had happened to me, and it still hurt keenly to think of them. Now, though, I could look back on my former self with a sort of pity. To me, that was the kind of "pathos" Beethoven had in mind when he composed the *Pathétique*.

"Music for a wounded heart," I murmured, raising the cup of tea to my lips.

The river shimmered in the moonlight.

4

"How about some more tea? You should try a dash of milk in your next cup!"

I was still gazing vacantly out at the waters of the Kamo when I heard these words. I looked up to see the master holding a porcelain jug.

"Yes, please," I said, holding out my teacup.

"This is Astral Milk—fresh from the Milky Way," said the master, gazing up at the wispy band of light crossing the dark expanse of sky.

As the milk splashed into the cup, the amber-colored tea took on a pearly color.

"Even with tea, just adding milk creates a whole new drink . . ." I murmured.

"Indeed it does," the master said with a smile.

"Those things you were saying about the Moon,

51

and Mercury, and Venus . . . Maybe that's a bit like this tea."

"It is?"

"Yes. The cold water becomes hot water—and the leaves turn it into tea. Then the milk turns it into something completely different again. It goes through all these phases . . ." I said in a quiet voice.

The tortoiseshell cat chuckled. "That's a very creative interpretation! I'd expect nothing less from a scriptwriter of your caliber."

"Oh, please. I was just rambling!" I could feel myself flushing.

"But what you say does make a lot of sense. The tea starts out as water, but experience transforms it entirely."

"Just now, you said I hadn't 'properly completed' the previous phases of my life. What did you mean by that?"

The master nodded, then gestured toward the chair opposite me. "Mind if I take a seat?"

"Please," I replied. The human-sized chair looked a little cramped for the oversized tortoiseshell cat.

"You see," he said, settling into the chair, "there

are certain things you need to learn in each of the different phases, and if you haven't, then sometimes a bit of a 'crash course' may be necessary."

"Right . . ."

"For example, if you don't work things out with your parents during your Moon phase—when you're a child, in other words—that can cause rifts between you during your Sun phase in your late twenties. Or if you don't focus on your studies when you're at school in your Mercury phase, then you might end up playing catch-up during your Mars phase."

It was true: people who didn't get the chance to disobey their parents when they were young often seemed to have a delayed rebellious phase when they were older. As for his second example, I recalled an interview I'd once read with the president of a large corporation. He hadn't paid any attention at all in school, and started his company without even attending college. The more the company grew, the more he had to educate himself—a process that became a struggle in its own right. "Sooner or later," I remembered him commenting, "there comes a time in all our lives when we just have to sit down and *study*!"

The tuxedo cat walked back over and hopped up onto the table. "In that sense, Miss Serikawa, you got through your Moon phase and Mercury phase without any trouble."

Maybe it was because I'd been my parents' second daughter, but they kept me on a pretty loose leash, and I'd always felt able to speak my mind. And, as a reasonably sharp kid who liked being praised, I'd always been a good student. When my parents told me I'd make a good teacher, I'd been delighted.

At this point, the Singapura appeared and joined the other cats at the table, lying on his belly with his head propped on his paws.

"But then in your Venus phase . . . it seems you really focused on your hobbies—at the expense of romance?"

I flinched at these words. He wasn't wrong. Between the ages of sixteen and twenty-five, during my Venus phase, I'd devoted myself much more to my personal interests than to any serious pursuit of love. I'd always enjoyed writing novels, so I joined the literary club at university, where we published our own small magazine. Between that, my part-time job, and obsessively going to see my favorite actor at the theater, there wasn't much time left over for anything else. I'd always been much more interested in fictional love stories than in any romance of my own, and it wasn't until my fourth year of university that I fell in love.

I met him at a graduation party. By chance, we were the only two singles in the room. Someone who'd had a few too many drinks shouted, "You two should just date each other!" At the time, the two of us had grinned awkwardly at each other in commiseration. But not long afterward, we ended up going to see a film together.

I wasn't particularly drawn to him physically, but we had the same interests and he was a pretty relaxing person to be around. Soon enough, we were an item.

We'd been together six years when he proposed. Apparently, his boss and parents had been telling him it was time to settle down. But, preoccupied by my scriptwriting work, I found myself unable to say yes. And so we went our separate ways.

After that, I got to know a younger man who

worked as an assistant director for a regional television network, and before long we were going out. In the end, we were together for almost a decade, during which time he slowly worked his way up the career ladder while I, on other hand, slid down and hit rock bottom.

In the last few years of our relationship, he must have gotten sick of me hinting at marriage whenever we met. He started contacting me less and less frequently. Then came those shocking words:

"I'm getting married."

To someone else, in other words.

And I thought I was his girlfriend!

I was deep in these negative thoughts when the tuxedo cat turned to me. "If you neglect your relationships, they'll always end that way. Things happen to us because we let them, Mizuki."

The cat had a point. Toward the end of that relationship, I'd become pretty self-absorbed. More precisely, I'd tried my best to ignore my boyfriend's behavior. I couldn't face up to the reality that he was growing increasingly distant.

Tears began trickling down my cheeks again.

"Hey, stop picking on the poor woman!" said the Singapura in a chiding tone.

The tuxedo cat wrinkled his nose. "I wasn't *picking* on her . . ."

"Well, you shouldn't be so blunt about stuff like this! Sorry, Miss Serikawa. He'll go and get you a little dessert as a way of saying sorry—won't you?"

"As you wish . . ." said the tuxedo cat, hopping down from the table and heading inside the café.

The master patted me on the back with his paw. "You had a peaceful Moon phase, a studious Mercury phase, and a fun-filled Venus phase, which was why you were able to shine so brightly during your Sun phase."

It was true that my Sun phase—the years between twenty-six and thirty-five, in other words—had been my golden years. Back then, it felt as if life was mine for the taking.

"Then . . . why am I like this now?" I asked, choking slightly on my tears.

The tortoiseshell let out a quiet sigh. "It's possible

that during your Sun phase, you shone so brightly that you dazzled yourself. There were certain lessons you were supposed to learn—but didn't."

"That's right," continued the Singapura. "You just kept on going, without ever stopping to wonder what it was that made your scripts so popular in the first place."

I flinched again at how accurate this description was.

The tortoiseshell waved a placating paw. "Right now, you're playing catch-up. The problem is, you still haven't been paying attention."

I was lost for words. I didn't quite know what he meant by "playing catch-up," but it was true that, for some time now, I'd been trying to ignore reality.

"So what should I do?" I asked, looking up at the cats.

"First off, you need to really know yourself," said the Singapura with a grin.

Easier said than done.

At this point, the tortoiseshell produced a pocket watch.

"Mind if I view your natal chart?"

"My . . . natal chart?" I asked, raising an eyebrow.

"You see, as well as running this place, I also read people's stars."

"Oh. You mean like . . . astrology?"

"Exactly," the tortoiseshell said with a nod.

"Right," I said with a shrug.

I was a Pisces by the skin of my teeth. If I'd been born a day later, I'd have been an Aries. Maybe that was why my horoscope never seemed to tally with reality.

"When I say reading your stars, I don't mean the kind of fortune-telling you might be thinking of. Instead, I will use your natal chart to carefully analyze your records."

"My . . . records?" I asked blankly.

"Yes," said the master. "So can I take a look at your chart?"

I nodded.

"Right, then," said the master. Then, after holding his pocket watch up to my forehead briefly, he withdrew it again and opened up its case. I peered

59

inside and saw that, rather than an ordinary watch face, the interior was filled with astrological dials.

The master pushed the winding crown. The surface of the "watch" shone brightly. I looked up. Projected onto the night sky was an enormous horoscope.

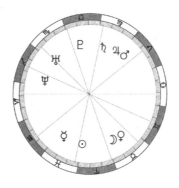

I gasped at the huge chart filling the sky.

"What does this . . . tell you?" I asked.

"Why, everything there is to know about you."

The master seemed to sense my doubt. Squinting up at the sky, he launched into an explanation. "Western astrology is said to have originated in Babylonia in the second millennium BC. That's about four thousand years ago."

"It was developed that long ago?"

"It can all seem a little ancient, I know. People back then might not have known as much as we do now, but in a sense they were just as wise. Human knowledge is a remarkable thing. After all, its gradual accumulation is what enabled humans to travel into space, isn't it? Our ancestors' knowledge of space was a little different. Rather than aiming for the stars, they sought to understand them. For them, astrology wasn't fortune-telling but genuine scholarship—a science, in other words. Astrology doesn't show us how to travel into space; it is a compass that, drawing on the wisdom of the universe, shows us both our past and our future.

"Your natal chart, meanwhile, reveals your most fundamental attributes. Remember how just now you compared life to the journey taken by a cup of tea? Cold water becoming hot, hot water becoming tea, and so on? Well, different people start from different places. Some might start out as milk, not water. Or maybe something entirely different, like earth. For example, that earth might become clay, which might one day become a building," said the master, still looking up at the horoscope. "And this chart tells me whether you started as water, or milk, or earth."

"You mean it tells you my key characteristics?"

"Exactly!" exclaimed the Singapura, wagging a paw in my direction.

"Yes," said the master. "And that knowledge can be most revealing. For example, someone who was born as earth might realize that they'll never become a cup of tea, no matter how hard they try."

I burst out laughing at this strained analogy. "Well, yes, I guess that *would* be a stretch."

"Exactly," the master said with a nod. "Please, take another look at your natal chart."

I did as he said.

"See how the circle is divided into twelve houses, like a clock? This time, let's think of life as a plant. Half of it sits above the ground and the other half— the roots—in the soil."

"Right."

"As long as you make sure the roots are happy, the plant will produce beautiful flowers. And if it doesn't, then you only ever need to look at the roots."

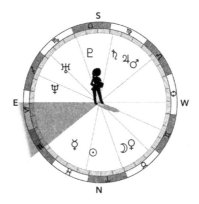

As the master said this, the bottom half of the horoscope glowed faintly.

"With horoscopes, the top part is south and the bottom is north. As we're looking at it, the left is east and the right is west. The first house starts on the eastern side, where the sun rises. It represents your self."

Now it was the first house that seemed to glow.

"My . . . self?"

"See that squiggly sign next to the 'east' marker? That's the symbol for Capricorn, where your first house begins. Capricorns are sensible, diligent, and studious. And they can't bear any kind of wrongdoing. Your natal chart also hints that you are quite ambitious."

I gulped. He wasn't wrong.

"But, Master," said the Singapura, pointing up at the horoscope. "Her first house becomes Aquarius halfway through, doesn't it?"

Counterclockwise from the Capricorn sign was another symbol, this one consisting of two wavy lines. That was Aquarius, then. The Water Bearer.

"In other words," continued the Singapura, "you also have an Aquarius side—the ability to calmly gather and analyze information."

"While we're on the subject," said the master, "let's talk a little more about Aquarius. After all, it'll be very important—for all of you."

"All of us?"

"Yes. Everyone alive today."

My eyes widened at his dramatic turn of phrase.

5

"Until recently, it was the Age of Pisces. Now, however, we've entered the Age of Aquarius."

I cocked my head. "The Age of Aquarius?"

"That's right," said the master, pushing the winding crown on his pocket watch again. "Among star readers, that refers to the precession of the Earth's vernal equinox from Pisces to Aquarius . . ."

The symbol of Pisces—two fish tied together with a string—appeared alongside the horoscope in the sky.

"You see, the Age of Pisces lasted for around two millennia, starting from around the birth of Christ."

"Two thousand years of . . . Pisces?"

"Yep," chipped in the Singapura, seeing the shocked look on my face. "Obviously. And after that it's another two thousand or so of Aquarius."

"You see, you're all bound up with Aquarius, whether you like it or not," the master continued.

So it would be the Age of Aquarius my whole life. In fact, even if I was reincarnated, it would still be the Age of Aquarius.

"The Age of Pisces was a time of duality and conflict, as illustrated by the two fish tied together. An age when societies were ruled by their dominant class, often in the form of an academic meritocracy— and everyone swam desperately in the same direction, trying to make their way to the top."

That sounded about right. Growing up, life had always seemed like a fight to the top. All anyone seemed to want was to attend a top-tier school and end up at a top-tier company.

"Are you saying things have changed now?"

The Singapura laughed wryly and scratched his head. "Not exactly. The effects of Pisces are still sort of . . . lingering. I mean, it might have given way to Aquarius, but you can't expect an age that's been around for two thousand years to just vanish without a trace, can you?"

The master nodded in agreement. "When the age changes, the effects of the previous one continue to linger for at least a decade. It's more of a gradual transition, you see."

"A gradual transition?" I smiled. "What will the Age of Aquarius be like, then?"

Just as the master was about to reply, the Singapura leaped onto the table, reared up on his back legs, and put a paw to his chest. "Hey, if it's Aquarius we're talking about, let *me* fill you in."

"Yes, perhaps Caelus can explain," said the master.

So the Singapura's name was Caelus. *What a weird name,* I thought.

"The big theme of Aquarius is revolution."

"Revolution . . . ?"

"Yeah. A complete transformation of the values inherited from the previous age. Unfortunately, that can set the stage for all kinds of disasters—whether natural or man-made. There isn't much we can do about it—it's all a part of the cosmic machine."

Now that I thought about it, all sorts of previously unthinkable incidents and natural disasters had been occurring in recent years.

"Cosmic or not," I found myself saying, "that sounds like a bit of a rough deal . . ."

The Singapura looked as crestfallen as if I'd criticized him personally.

"Actually, when revolution comes knocking, it's not the universe that decides what happens," said the master apologetically. "No, that part is up to mankind."

"Wait, *we're* the ones who decide?" I asked, frowning.

"How can I put this . . ." began the Singapura, a

little hesitantly. "Think of the revolution as an end-of-term test. Everything you've done up to that point is revealed in the results."

Maybe he'd chosen this analogy because he knew I used to be a teacher, but it went right over my head. I gave him a puzzled look.

The master chuckled again. "Think of the French Revolution. If the monarchy had been on better terms with the people, a great deal of bloodshed could have been avoided. It's the same with the up-heavals of recent years: now that we've entered an age of revolution, all sorts of problems that humans have spent decades trying to ignore have all erupted at once. The universe never said it had to be that way. If humans knew how to face up to their problems properly—if they could just manage to be a bit less *rigid* about everything—then a more peaceful revo-lution would be possible."

In an ideal world, what he was describing might be possible. But . . .

"But humans *don't* change, do they?" I found my-self saying. The master nodded in bitter agreement.

"That's why there's no such thing as a quiet revolution," said the Singapura. "They always feel like a blow to the head. Afterward, everyone just wants things to go back to the way they were. But there's no going back. Once a war breaks out, you're not getting your old life back."

All you could do was wait for the war to be over, then try to build a new world.

"So you see," continued the Singapura, "people have no choice but to reinvent their values. The world is leaving the Age of Pisces and entering the Age of Aquarius. We're moving from the age of the group, in which everyone aims for the same summit, to the age of the individual. And technology is what's taking us there. In the coming era, each of our voices will carry more and more weight. The development of the internet, and the fact that ordinary people can become famous and gain an audience overnight— those are all manifestations of Aquarius."

That explained the rise of "influencers" over the last decade, then.

"The individual has gained the right to speak out: it's an era of free speech. But that can also lead to disorder. The Age of Aquarius is a time of diverse coexistence, in which everyone gets to be themselves. Under Pisces, you had to get married at a certain age, bring up children—all that stuff. But with Aquarius, everyone gets to do their own thing."

I nodded in agreement, thinking of all the countries that had started recognizing same-sex marriage recently. That had to be symbolic of this new age, too.

"Aquarius symbolizes technology, but it also has a spiritual aspect. Radio waves and human thought might seem completely different, but really they go hand in hand."

This was getting pretty deep.

"See, there was nothing inherently *wrong* with the Age of Pisces. It was a time of longing and dreaming, partly because the harsher conditions meant people were always yearning for a better life. In fact, the American dream is a real Pisces sort of story."

The master nodded in agreement. "Or Cinderella— I suppose that's rather Piscean, too."

I clapped my hands together. It was all starting to make sense. Of course: the diligent and hardworking heroine who puts everything on the line and ends up winning the heart of a high-society prince. Based on what I'd heard, that did sound pretty Piscean. And now that I thought about it, I'd penned plenty of stories like that.

My eyes widened. "You know, a lot of my shows were just like that."

At this, a smile spread across the master's face.

"They certainly were," the Singapura said with a nod of agreement. "When your dramas were first aired, the world was still steeped in the effects of Pisces, even though it had entered the Age of Aquarius. Deep down, the public knew that times were changing—but they couldn't resist the occasional throwback from the previous era."

So that was why people had liked my shows so much. Then, when the influence of Pisces finally waned, they'd lost all interest in them.

"Nobody needs them anymore, do they?" I said. "Times really have changed . . ."

"Not exactly!"

I turned around to find the tuxedo cat holding a tray. On it was a glass vessel with two handles—just like the Aquarius sign.

"It's just like those life phases we discussed earlier," he continued, setting the jug down on the table. Inside it was what looked like an English trifle. From the side, I could make out various layers of custard, sponge cake, and fruit through the glass.

"It is?"

"Yes. Each age contains lessons that we take into the next. Rather than discarding the Age of Pisces entirely, we carry it inside us. Remember those two fish that were tied together? Well, now they've been released from their bonds and swim freely—in this fetching Aquarian jug."

I could make out a fish-shaped jelly bobbing around in the glass jug, as though it was swimming inside the trifle.

"Think about it. People have loved classical music for a long time, and they'll carry on doing so," said the master. "In the same way, there'll always be a demand for Cinderella-type stories."

The tuxedo cat nodded. "You just have to tweak them a little. You know, make them a bit more ... Aquarian."

Classical music had always been performed differ-

THE FULL MOON COFFEE SHOP

ently depending on the period in question. Why shouldn't it be the same for stories?

"Now, let's have one more look at your natal chart," said the master, gazing up at the horoscope in the night sky. "As I said earlier, life is like a plant—if you want things to go well, you have to take care of your roots. Now, the first house is that of the self. The second relates to possessions and money—you see how you have Mercury in there?"

"Mercury is all about information, transmission, and timing," the Singapura chipped in.

"Intelligence and communication, too," the tuxedo cat said. "In terms of star signs, meanwhile, your second house straddles Aquarius and Pisces. Your chosen professions—teaching and scriptwriting—both seem like fitting careers for you. The fact that you ultimately settled on scriptwriting may be down to your Piscean ability to channel your imagination into your creative work."

"But then why are things going so badly for me these days?"

"Hmm," said the master, squinting as if to think.

"As I said, there's nothing wrong with the profession you've chosen. Which means that the real root of the problem must lie in the Home. That's the fourth house. For you that's associated with Taurus—and in there you have the Moon, which is associated with our inner self, and Venus."

At this, the Singapura and the tuxedo cat both nodded their heads sagely. "Makes sense," said the Singapura.

"Sorry, *what* makes sense?"

"Taurus is a symbol of fertility, or abundance," explained the master. "In relation to the Home, it denotes a space of luxury. You have the Moon and Venus in that house. That means that if you want to produce your best work, you need a home where your inner self can truly relax. If you don't, you'll feel miserable, and things will only go from bad to worse. In other words, for you, home has to be a sanctuary."

Something deep within me clicked into place.

When my ratings had begun to plummet and I'd started skipping out on my job, sacrificing my only source of income, I'd ended up ditching the apartment I loved for a place whose only merit was that it was cheap.

"But . . . I couldn't afford my old apartment anymore!" I exclaimed, looking down and clenching my fists on my lap. "And it's not like I can even think about moving house right now."

I hadn't *wanted* to leave my old apartment; I'd been *forced* to. I was beginning to feel as if the cats were being a little flippant.

"If you'd really decided you weren't going to budge, are you sure you couldn't have found a way to keep your old place? Isn't it just that you were feeling pretty desperate about everything at the time?"

His words were harsh, but also true. More than anything, I *had* been desperate—reckless, even. That was why I'd sold all my good furniture, too—I felt I didn't deserve it anymore.

"We're not saying you need to move somewhere new," said the tuxedo cat. "Instead, you should strive to make your current home as comfortable a place to live and work as possible."

The master smiled in agreement. "He's right.

75

The important part is the *realization* that what you really need is a relaxing home. That will lead naturally to a decision to do everything you can to make it a reality one day. Gaining that truer understanding of yourself—that's what really matters."

I'd been living in an apartment I hated, with furniture I'd bought as cheaply as possible. I'd turned myself into the heroine from some tragedy. It was as if I was trying to prove to someone just how low I could go—giving up everything I enjoyed; eating instant food to save money; and consciously avoiding the cafés that had been my havens. I'd been leading as shabby and miserable an existence as I could manage. Somewhere in the back of my mind, I was probably hoping my invitation to the ball would magically turn up one day.

But what I really needed, if I ever wanted my ticket to that ball, was to live as comfortably and peacefully as I could in the present. Rather than living in the past and the possible future.

"You know, ever since I was a kid, I've always liked decorating my room—turning it into my own special space."

THE FULL MOON COFFEE SHOP

The master's eyes narrowed as he smiled. "Understand yourself, and you'll be able to care for yourself. As long as you do that, you'll shine like the star that you are."

"The star that I am?"

"Humans are stars in their own right, Mizuki. Every one of them."

I looked up at the night sky and closed my eyes.

My thoughts drifted to my current apartment. It could be a whole lot nicer if I just put my mind to it. The thought alone gave me a thrill of excitement.

When I opened my eyes again, the master and the Singapura had disappeared. They must have gone back inside the café. Only the tuxedo cat remained. He poured some more tea into my empty cup, then beamed at me.

"Please. *Do* enjoy the trifle!"

It was the first time I'd seen him smile. It felt as if he'd given me a precious gift.

Delighted, I reached for my spoon.

The tuxedo cat began walking back toward the café.

"By the way . . ." I said. He stopped and turned. "What's your name?"

"My name? You can call me Cronus."

"Cronus . . ."

It was just as strange and impressive a name as the Singapura's. But it, too, sounded vaguely familiar. The tuxedo cat bowed and disappeared into the café.

I stuck my spoon into the trifle and tried a mouthful. The cream, fruit, and jelly all melted together in my mouth, each asserting its flavor without drowning the others out. A real Aquarian dessert. Eating something *this* delicious and under a star-filled sky: it was a moment of pure joy.

"That was so good," I murmured when I'd polished off the trifle. The stars were twinkling away above me.

I remembered taking the children to a planetarium when I was a teacher. We'd learned about all the different gods the planets were named after. I always thought the English word "Saturn" sounded like "Satan," but at the planetarium we learned that the name actually came from the Roman god Saturnus.

. . . Or, as he was known in Greece, Cronus.

In other words, the tuxedo cat was . . . Saturn?

I glanced over at the café. But it was no longer there.

6

"Excuse me, madam!"

A gentle female voice called out to me.

My eyes snapped open. A glittering chandelier came into view, together with a woman wearing a black dress and a white apron, looking worriedly at me.

"Are you feeling okay?"

I was sprawled on a comfortable sofa. On the table in front of me was an empty coffee cup.

Slowly regaining my senses, I realized I was still in the hotel café. I must have dozed off.

"Sorry," I said, hastily getting to my feet. "I, er . . ."

"Don't worry," said the waitress, shaking her head. "Would you like another coffee before you go?"

I felt even more embarrassed by her fussing over me. I shook my head and hurried out of the hotel.

I can't believe myself sometimes, I thought as I paced down the street. In fact, I'd have quite liked a coffee to help me wake up. But I'd been too proud to accept it.

Well, having Taurus in your first house can make you that way.

As this thought flitted across my mind, a smile spread across my face. I still vividly remembered everything I'd learned in my dream.

It had been quite the mysterious dream. A stargazing cat who ran a café, Cronus the tuxedo cat, and Caelus the Singapura . . .

Wait—what if Caelus was the name of a planet, too? I stopped and got my phone out. It turned out Caelus was the Roman equivalent of Uranus. Of course! Uranus—the planet of revolutionary change.

So . . . I'd actually met Saturn and Uranus? I gulped and looked up at the sky. Unlike in my dreams, there was only a smattering of stars out this evening.

Had it really just been a dream?

I couldn't forget the cats' words. After the Age of Pisces came the Age of Aquarius. The age of spirituality—and the internet. A time when the individual was truly respected. In an era like that, maybe I was lucky to be writing game scripts. Maybe this was actually an opportunity—one I shouldn't let slide.

Even if I wasn't allowed to include any breathtaking love scenes, I could still write wonderful stories. Instead of just aiming for average, I'd create the best side characters I could. As long as they made people feel as if they were edging closer to a blissful romance with the main character, then as a writer, I'd have done my job.

And what did I need in order to do it well?

Well, for now, I thought, *I'll buy some flowers on my way home. Maybe some nice cups and saucers . . .*

And after I'd decorated the room with the flowers, I'd make myself a nice cup of tea—and get to work.

Then, one day, with a bit of luck, I'd be able to visit the Full Moon Coffee Shop one more time.

Maybe then they'd make me that cup of coffee.

I made my way down Kawaramachi Street with a spring in my step—and the hint of a smile on my face.

CHAPTER 2

LUNAR CHOCOLATE FONDANT

AKARI NAKAYAMA

1

I shouldn't have met her in person, I realized as I gazed vacantly out of the office window.

I was sitting in a meeting room inside the television station. I'd arrived a little ahead of schedule, so I was sitting by the window, my latte from the café still in my hand, replaying in my head the encounter I'd just had.

I'm sorry, Mizuki—they turned it down.

I could still see the look on her face when I'd said those words.

I'd had to break it to her that the scripts that she—the former "hitmaker"—wrote just weren't relevant to audiences anymore.

I should have just told her in writing. In fact, I'd initially intended to break the news by email. But when I remembered I was coming to Kyoto on business, I couldn't resist the chance to see her again.

It wasn't just her past successes that made me think so highly of her. There was another reason—something very trivial, really. I'd always meant to tell her about it if I could find the chance—and yet, to this day, I never had. Mizuki had been my teacher at primary school.

"I basically handed her a death sentence," I murmured.

"Don't you mean you're *about* to?" came a voice from my side.

Startled, I turned around to find Jiro, a stylist I

often ran into here. The door to the meeting room was wide open. He must have seen me and wandered in.

"In a bit of a pickle, are you? Your lead actress goes and gets herself caught having an affair . . . That *is* why you're here, isn't it?"

Jiro was in his early forties, and always spoke with a lilt. He had a sculpted beard and longish, slightly curled hair that he'd casually tied back.

Despite our familiarity, I didn't know his last name. Everyone just called him Jiro-san.

He always knew how to read a situation. As a result, he seemed to be popular with almost everyone he met. There was something about him that put me on edge, though I'd never been able to put my finger on what it was.

"Well, yes, that's why I'm here, but . . ."

"But?"

"I met up with Mizuki Serikawa just now."

"Mizuki Serikawa? The scriptwriter?"

I nodded.

"Wow!" exclaimed Jiro, putting his hands to his cheeks in excitement. "I *adore* her work. Does that mean we're finally getting another one of her dramas?"

I averted my gaze. "I'm afraid not," I said quietly.

"Oh," he said, adjusting his tone accordingly. "So *that's* what you meant by 'death sentence' . . . "

I nodded again. "I hadn't heard from her in ages, then she sent me this pitch out of the blue . . ."

"And it was no good?"

"I wouldn't say that, exactly . . . In fact, it wasn't bad, so I showed it to the execs. But they weren't convinced. 'Out of touch with the times' was their verdict . . ."

"Oh, dear," said Jiro gently. "Tricky, isn't it? Sometimes the retro thing can go down pretty well with audiences, but I guess it only works if you go all out with it. Otherwise it's sort of like a café that can't decide whether it's an old-school coffee shop or a trendy hipster joint." He paused. "But you still went to the effort of meeting her, instead of just breaking it to her by email. Was there some other reason you wanted to see her?"

He'd hit the bull's-eye again.

It was true: really, I'd met her in person because there was something I wanted to know. I wanted to see if Mizuki Serikawa still had that *spark*.

Some people hate the word "ambition," but success never lasts long without it. Ambition means being committed to your job. It means being serious about what you do and how you go about achieving it.

When Mizuki was at the forefront of our industry, I could always see that ambition in her eyes—a sparkling excitement for everything she did.

If she'd hit a slump and the executives had gone cold on her pitches, well, that was that. It was the kind of thing that could happen to anyone—which was why I'd hoped to still see that hunger in her eyes. But, after meeting her, I could tell her spark had gone—and it had floored me.

"I told Mizuki her pitch had been rejected," I murmured, half to myself. "And sure, she looked a bit shocked—but then she just chuckled and left it at that. The old Mizuki would have turned right around and said, 'So, tell me: how can I make it work?'—but there was none of that."

"What a shame," said Jiro, folding his arms. "Well, Akari, I see you're as ruthless as ever!"

"Ruthless?"

My colleagues had made comments like this before, but I didn't remember ever showing Jiro this side of me. Yet here he was, making it out to be common knowledge. I wondered if there were negative rumors going around about me.

Jiro chuckled. "Oh, don't worry—no one's gossiping about you being some kind of tyrant. It's just that, as a neutral observer, I get the impression that you can be pretty tough on yourself as well as on others."

"Jiro, you come across all gentle and nice, but you're a sharp one, aren't you?"

"People tell me that," he said, nodding and looking at his hands.

"You know, I have a close friend who's a hairdresser and she's just like you. She seems all soft around the edges, but she has this amazing ability to read people. Are you beauty-industry types all like that?"

He let out a little burst of laughter. "I'm not sure about that, but I guess we do spend all day looking at people. You know, trying to see them for who they really are. Maybe that's where we get our powers of observation from."

The best stylists and hairdressers were the ones

who focused not just on your looks but on what you really wanted to be and project as a person. No wonder they were so perceptive.

"So," continued Jiro, "does this friend of yours always do your hair?"

"No, actually. She lives here in Kyoto, where I grew up, whereas I'm based in Tokyo these days. So I don't often get the chance to see her."

"Ooh, I didn't realize you were a Kyotoite! I always thought of you as a Tokyo type ..."

"My parents are both from the Tokyo area, but my dad's job meant that we lived in Kyoto while I was in primary and middle school. That's when I met my friend."

"That makes sense," replied Jiro, folding his arms. "So, is she any good? I was actually thinking I could do with a bit of help on the hairdressing front ..."

"Yeah, she's good. Used to work at a famous salon in Osaka. But she ended up quitting because she didn't quite fit in with the place. Now she just works at a beauty parlor run by her parents. She seems pretty happy there."

"Does she now! Well, I guess that rules me out."

"I'll tell her you're looking for a hairdresser. Just in case."

"Thanks. Hey, we should swap contact details! Here's my QR code," said Jiro, handing over his business card.

"Thanks," I said, scanning it with my phone and saving him as a contact.

"Finally got your number," he said with a grin. "Lucky me!"

I looked away, flustered, then tried to change the subject.

"Jiro, going back to what you were saying . . ."

"What did I say?"

"You know, about how ruthless I can be."

"Ah," he said with a nod.

"Was that because I met up with Mizuki just to tell her that her pitch was no good?"

On reflection, it *had* been pretty harsh of me. Feeling a little sick with myself, I looked down at my feet.

"Oh, no, not that. I mean, if she'd convinced you that she really wanted the job, I'm sure you'd have worked something out with her. But when you told her the pitch was no good, she gave up on the spot, right?"

I nodded.

"And you saw that and thought, Well, if *that's* how little she cares, then what does it matter? Right?"

"I guess so."

I hadn't stopped to pick apart my thoughts at the time, but it was pretty hard to argue with Jiro's analysis.

"*That's* the part I thought was a little harsh."

"Do you think I made the wrong decision, though?"

"That's not the point. I bet Mizuki summoned up every ounce of her courage to send you that pitch."

"Oh, definitely." *All the more reason not to give up so easily,* I thought.

"When you put yourself out there like that and get a straight-up rejection, it can really floor you. Unless you're naturally confident, sticking to your guns is *hard.*"

I thought back to the high-spirited Mizuki I used to know. A "no" had never stopped her—she'd bounce right back, asking how she could make it work, and refuse to give up. She could be pretty demanding sometimes, but I'd always respected that.

But Jiro had made me realize something. If she was able to act like that back then, it was probably because she was shielded by a layer of self-confidence——the kind that came from actually getting results and being respected.

I fell silent.

"Still," said Jiro, crossing his arms again, "you're not exactly wrong. After plucking up her courage and finally landing a meeting with you, she probably shouldn't have let the chance just slip through her fingers."

I could tell he was trying to console me.

"Still, the two of you are pretty close, right? Let me guess——you were a fan of hers once upon a time."

"Oh, definitely. But there's another reason, too . . ."

"Another reason?"

"The two of us go way back."

"Ooh. Why's that?"

"I knew her before she became famous. She probably doesn't remember me from back then, but I remember her, all right. She taught me about the importance of helping people, you see. That was partly why I was so keen to give her a hand . . ."

I didn't expect Mizuki to realize just how far back we went. But to me, she'd been such a beacon of kindness that I'd never been able to forget her.

"Go on then—what's the story?"

Just as Jiro leaned forward to listen, close enough that I could smell his amber scent, there was a voice from the door. "Akari?"

I looked up to find a man in a suit peering into the room. Takumi Tsukada—a media sales executive in his thirties who was probably here to discuss the fallout from the actress's scandal, too. It must have been at least six months since we'd last seen each other. I worked in Tokyo most of the time, whereas he'd moved to Kyoto after his agency had assigned him the west of the country.

In the past, we'd meet for a meal or a drink whenever I came this way on business. In other words, once upon a time, we'd dated.

"Ooh," said Jiro, "Mr. Tsukada—looking very sharp as always, if you don't mind me saying!"

Takumi laughed and gave a self-effacing shake of the head.

"I hear you'll be a father soon," continued Jiro. "Congratulations to you and your wife!"

Takumi bowed a little hesitantly, then glanced at me. "Akari—could we talk for a moment?"

"Sorry. I have a meeting starting now."

"It'll only take five minutes," he said, clasping his hands together.

"I'm afraid I really don't have the time," I replied in a brusque tone, not meeting his gaze. My hands were quivering on my lap.

"I see." Takumi frowned, then walked off. Once he'd disappeared from view, my shoulders drooped with relief.

Jiro put his hands on his hips and said, "There's history between you two, I take it?"

I clammed up.

"Had a little fling, did we?"

I looked sharply up. "It's not like that! I didn't

even know about his wife. He's got a metal allergy, which means he can't wear a ring, and he never mentioned her . . . so . . ."

I trailed off mid-sentence, surprised by how much I'd already confessed. Other than my hairdresser friend, I'd never told anyone about this. It was absurd to have blurted all that out—and to Jiro, of all people!

"So you ended up dating him without even realizing he was married?"

"Well . . . I wouldn't say we were dating," I said, looking down to hide the tears in my eyes.

"Ah. I get it," said Jiro. "That must have been tough. Especially for someone like you. Well, if you ever need a friendly ear, I'm here."

He laid his hand on my shoulder. I couldn't even get out a reply.

A second later, the show director and production staff came into the meeting room.

"Well, I'll be off," said Jiro with a brisk wave. "Hang in there!"

On his way out, he passed Satsuki Ayukawa, the

lead actress who'd caused such a stir, walking into the room. She was in her mid-twenties. More the "cute" type than traditionally beautiful, she had a winning smile that had captured viewers' hearts. That was until a few days ago, when a tabloid had published an article revealing her affair with a married actor. Her adoring fans suddenly turned. A pile-on began, with the affair being dissected on television and social media on an hourly basis.

It was clearly taking its toll on her. She'd always been a lively, cheerful sort, but now she was barely recognizable. Her face was pallid, her expression dark; her skin and hair had lost their usual luster. It was like she'd aged five years overnight. She used to come into work with a chipper "Goo-ood morning!" but today all we got was a faint "Morning" as she sank into her chair.

She must have known what we were about to tell her: that she'd been fired from the role. I could see her hands tightly clenched together in her lap.

"Akari, could you start?" murmured the director in my ear. I nodded gravely, preparing to give my second death sentence of the day.

2

With the meeting over, I paced down the office corridor. I had a bad taste in my mouth, like I was about to throw up. Forcing a smile in the direction of each employee I passed, I made my way out of the building as quickly as I could.

Outside, I could breathe again.

It was some time after sunset and already quite dark. Still, I was on Karasuma, one of Kyoto's bigger avenues. Plenty of cars were passing, and the restaurants that lined the street were bustling with customers.

Across the avenue was Kyoto Gyoen, the imperial gardens. A little to the south was Marutamachi Station, where I'd been planning to catch a train straight back to my hotel. But my feelings were still in chaos.

Maybe a walk will do me good.

And so I made my way into the gardens.

Despite its austere appearance, Kyoto Gyoen was still a public park—and open around the clock, meaning you could stroll through it whenever you liked. It was a spacious, green place, filled with forests, lawns, ponds, and Shinto shrines. There was even a flea market there some days. But now, with night encroaching, there was barely anyone about, and silence reigned. As I wandered, I couldn't help recalling what had happened in the meeting room.

Satsuki Ayukawa had burst into tears before launching into the kind of apology you normally heard at a press conference. "I'm deeply sorry for all the trouble I've caused. I accept full responsibility for what happened. I should have known better."

When I told her that pressure from our sponsors meant we had no choice but to drop her from the show, all she said was "I knew it," before bursting into tears again.

"Listen," she said, her gaze still on her lap, "I know I was in the wrong. But why is it only me everyone's going after? I mean, I can understand his wife and kids being angry. But what about all these other people who it has nothing to do with? It's not like I've done anything to them! Anyway, the world is full of people having affairs—what makes me worse than anyone else? From the way everyone's carrying on, you'd think I'd killed someone! Why am I the one being persecuted?"

All this must have been building up inside her for a while. Once she'd said her piece, she dashed out of the room in tears.

Her manager rushed after her, but, it seemed, was unable to stop her. We sat there waiting until a message came in from him: "Satsuki seems to have gone back to her hotel already, so I'm afraid we're done here. Very sorry, everyone." And so we'd been forced to call it a day.

There was one thing she'd said that had really touched a nerve.

What makes me worse than anyone else?

From somewhere nearby came the distinct sound of a hiccup. I looked up from deep within my thoughts. The noise seemed to have come from a woman slumped on a nearby bench. It was too dark to see properly, but she looked as if she might be crying.

Just then, the woman produced a can of beer from the convenience-store shopping bag at her side, cracked it open, and took a long swig. She seemed to be drinking at quite a pace. A case of the post-breakup blues, maybe?

Not wanting to get involved, I decided to clear off. But just as I was about to turn on my heels, something stopped me.

The wind picked up, parting the thick clouds and revealing a large full moon. The scene was suddenly illuminated. I got a better look at the woman on the bench—and realized who she was.

Satsuki Ayukawa.

"Satsuki . . . !" I blurted.

"Huhhh?" she said, turning in my direction. "Oh! Akari Nakayama, as I live and breathe! Gr-great work today—really . . ."

She came reeling in my direction—then fell straight onto her backside.

"Are you okay?" I asked, rushing over and carefully helping her to her feet. "Your manager must be worried about you, you know."

"I doubt it. It's not like I have anything on the

calendar anymore . . ." She spread her arms wide, giggled to herself, and began twirling around on the spot.

"Erm . . . Satsuki, are you sure you're okay?" I asked, catching her.

"Look at me, Akari. Drunk, on my own, in an empty park at night. Do you really think I'm okay? And I always thought you were a bright spark . . ."

Watching her put a hand to her mouth as she began tittering again, I felt my patience wearing thin.

"Guess I don't need to worry after all," I said, beginning to walk off.

"Hey, Akari, what's this about you and a married man?"

My heart leaped into my mouth.

"I arrived early for the meeting, you see. I was taking a rest in the room next door, but when I walked past yours on my way to the bathroom, I overheard you and Jiro chatting. So . . . you're no better than me, huh? And then you have the nerve to turn to me and tell me *I've* been dropped?"

"I'm *not* having an affair!" I cried out, in a voice that seemed to come from somewhere deep inside

me. It must have been pretty alarming, because Satsuki suddenly shrank away from me. "Seriously—
I'm not," I said, holding my head in my hands. "I'm
not having an affair."

"Okay, okay . . ." murmured Satsuki. She seemed
to be sobering up slightly.

Just then, I noticed something glimmering softly
in the corner of my eye. We both turned to look at the
source of the light. Below a large tree stood what
looked like a food truck of some kind. It must have
just arrived.

A young woman in a dark navy apron was putting
out various sets of tables and chairs, together with a
sign that read: THE FULL MOON COFFEE SHOP.

"They're opening a café at this time of night?" I
said. "Weird."

"Yeah, that *is* weird."

We glanced at each other instinctively. When we
looked back at the truck, the woman had disappeared.
In her place was a snow-white Persian cat, who
seemed to be looking at us—and gesturing with one
paw for us to come over.

3

惑星アイスのアフォガード

In the middle of the otherwise deserted park, the Full Moon Coffee Shop was bathed in moonlight. The café gave off a gentle glow.

The delicious fragrance of coffee—the kind that normally wafted from charming old-fashioned cafés—emanated from within. The Persian cat was still looking in our direction. It even seemed to be wearing a dark navy apron, as if to match the one the woman had been wearing. The smell of coffee and the cat's enigmatic gaze were impossible to resist. I turned to Satsuki and said, "How about getting a coffee? That should sober you up . . ."

We found ourselves drifting toward the Full Moon

Coffee Shop, as though pulled in by a mysterious force. As we approached, the Persian cat opened its mouth as if to meow. But instead, out came the word "Welcome."

We stopped in our tracks, our eyes widening in surprise. Was it some kind of ventriloquist act? I found myself glancing at the truck. From the window behind the small counter, a tuxedo cat was looking stiffly over at us.

"Is this one of those cat cafés, do you think?" I said.

"Weird, isn't it?" replied Satsuki, grasping my arm in fright. "I mean, I swear that cat just talked." Then she leaned in close and murmured, "I reckon this is one of those pranks you see on chat shows! Let's just play along with it, okay?"

Of course. It had to be a prank. What other explanation could there be? I felt embarrassed, as someone who worked in the television industry, for not having noticed quicker.

Satsuki, meanwhile, carried on pretending to be amazed, playing to her assumed audience. She really was a pro. With role after role evaporating in the wake of the adultery scandal, she was probably delighted to be receiving attention—even in the form of a prank.

Seeing our shocked faces, the Persian cat chuckled. "Sorry if I surprised you. I'm Venus, and I work here at the Full Moon Coffee Shop. The master of the café is away at the moment, but I—and my colleague Cronus over there—will be delighted to serve you this evening."

A Persian cat named Venus . . . The more I gazed at her shimmering golden eyes, the more they looked like miniature versions of the planet that was her namesake. As for that beautiful voice of hers, it was presumably being supplied by some actor concealed backstage and played out of a speaker hidden in her apron. Cats weren't known for their acting skills, though. Maybe it was a very realistic robot? Technology these days was really something . . .

"Could we get a coffee?" I asked.

The Persian cat gave me an apologetic smile. "I'm afraid we don't actually take orders from our customers."

"What? We can't order anything?" asked Satsuki. This time, the surprise in her voice was genuine.

"That's right," continued the Persian. "Instead, we pick out a selection of drinks, snacks, and desserts just for you."

"Right," I said with a nod. "So it's a sort of . . . tailored gourmet experience?"

"Indeed. Now, please take a seat. The two of you go way back, don't you? I'm sure you have plenty to talk about. Oh, and I can assure you that there are no cameras running—so just relax and enjoy yourselves."

Flashing a mischievous grin, the cat placed two glasses of water on the table, then disappeared into the café.

"Did you hear that? She said there aren't any cameras!" I said, startled.

"She probably just meant they'll pause filming until our drinks get here," responded Satsuki casually, settling into her chair and taking a sip of water. "Anyway, it's not like anyone's actually going to fall for a talking cat. It must be one of those pranks where they expect us to go along with it anyway."

I gave her a puzzled look as I settled into the chair opposite her.

"But what did she mean about us going way back, I wonder?"

At this, Satsuki giggled. "So you never realized?"

"Realized what?"

"We were at primary school together."

My eyes widened in surprise. Now that I thought about it, Satsuki *had* grown up in Kyoto. But . . .

"I'm not surprised you don't remember me. Satsuki Ayukawa's my stage name. And I tended to sort of fade into the background as a kid."

I leaned forward, unable to hide my amazement. "So . . . were we friends back then?"

She shook her head. "No, I was the year below you, so we didn't really know each other. But I remember you because we were in the same walk-to-school group, and you were the group leader."

If we were in different years, maybe it wasn't that surprising that I didn't remember Satsuki. Still, whatever she might claim, a star like her would surely have stood out—even as a child. And yet I just couldn't place her . . .

Seeing the downcast look on my face as I trawled through my memories, Satsuki laughed. "Oh, I was a little chubbier back then. In fact, I held up our entire group because I walked so slowly."

"Ah!" I exclaimed, finally remembering the plump girl who'd been a year below me at school. "That was you? Satsuki, you've really changed."

"When I started high school, I decided I was fed up with looking like that, so I took up jogging. It was the one sport that didn't cost any money, see."

Now that she mentioned it, she did have a toned, athletic sort of body—one that made for an appealing contrast with her bubbly personality. I remembered then that she had even published books on how to shape up.

She chuckled nostalgically. "Meanwhile, you haven't changed a bit—still the model student, aren't you!"

Embarrassed, I sipped my water.

"And yet you ended up making the same mistake as me. How come? Did you just get tired of always playing it straight?"

I frowned. "I'm telling you, it's not like that. I didn't do what you're . . . implying!"

Remembering that we might be on camera, I stopped short of saying the word "affair" out loud.

And yet every part of me wanted to shout: *I didn't have an affair!*

"Satsuki, can I ask you something?"

"Of course."

I nodded and gathered my thoughts. "Right. Well, was it like that with you? You got sick of playing the Goody Two-shoes and . . . deliberately went astray?"

Satsuki gave me a puzzled look, then sank her chin into her hands. "You know, I grew up without a father. It was pretty tough. TV became a sort of escape from reality for me. That was when I was happiest— sitting in front of the television. The world of showbiz had this sort of magnetic pull on me."

She sighed. "And he . . . he was exactly how I'd always imagined the perfect father. Of course, he wasn't my actual dad—which I guess was what made me so attracted to him. Someone working in the entertainment industry, who *also* happened to be exactly the kind of man who'd been missing my whole life—it was everything I'd ever wanted, and I couldn't put on the brakes. When I fell for him, I fell hard. I practically forgot he even had a family. I was too happy to think about anything that might come between us. . . .

And now the reality of it is hitting me. You know why I didn't have a dad? Because he ran off with some other woman, leaving my mom in the lurch. I hated that mistress of his with a passion—and now I've gone and followed in her footsteps. . . ."

Tears were streaming down Satsuki's face. Maybe they were only for the cameras. But something told me this was coming from her heart.

•   •   •

My own situation had been a little different.

Takumi Tsukada had moved to Kyoto temporarily for work, leaving his family behind. When he made his first move, he'd given the impression that he was completely single.

He was a media sales executive for a major advertising agency, with the stylish, whip-smart persona to match. I found him stimulating, and a few meals together were enough to make me fall for him. When he invited me back to his place for a drink one night, I said yes in a heartbeat.

I was on the cusp of my thirties, and marriage was

very much on my mind. If things worked out with him, I could tell he'd make a great partner—the type who'd be happy to marry a career woman like me. And his own position would be music to my parents' ears.

So yes, I was serious about him.

There was just one thing worrying me. Takumi was courteous, clever, and physically attractive. A magnet for women, in other words. What if he was seeing someone else at the same time as me?

But when I walked into the short-term rental apartment where he lived alone, I could detect no trace of any other woman. I felt a wave of relief. That night, we laid out the fancy snacks we'd picked up from a department-store food hall, clinked our wine-glasses together, and began chatting. My old colleague Mizuki Serikawa came up in our conversation. When I told him she'd been my teacher at primary school, his eyes shone with excitement.

"What do you mean? Was she giving some kind of scriptwriting class?"

"No, she was just a regular teacher back then. Actually, she was a substitute, so it wasn't like she was

111

my main teacher. But she used to accompany us home from school . . ."

After we'd chuckled together at the story, our conversation suddenly petered out. *Notting Hill,* a film I'd watched more times than I could count, was on the television—it was more like background noise than anything else. It was then that he drew me to him and brought his lips to mine. We began kissing, and before long he had pushed me down onto the floor. The weight of him, a faint quiver of panic— and alongside it, a ripple of pure ecstasy . . .

Just then his phone started vibrating. He'd turned the ringtone off, but even the sound of it buzzing around on the table was enough to shatter the mood.

"Your phone's ringing."

"Don't worry," he said, clearly irked. "It'll just be my boss calling me after he's had a few drinks."

Yet something in his expression bothered me. The phone call had been from a woman. I could just tell.

"It might be important. You should answer."

As I was about to hand him his phone, my eyes landed on the message he'd just received.

This morning sickness is killing me. I can't sleep. You're out with your colleagues tonight, right? Don't drink too much, okay? Urgh, wish I was allowed to drink. Pregnancy, childbirth, breastfeeding—this baby thing is a real slog, isn't it . . .

Just remembering the message sent a shiver down my spine. Talk about plunging straight from heaven into hell . . .

• • •

"Awful, right?" I said, smiling at my own idiocy as I finished telling Satsuki my story. "Those six lines of text told me everything I needed to know."

So Takumi was married—and his wife pregnant. I found out later that she'd been staying at her parents' home because her morning sickness was so bad. And, without knowing any of this, I had barged my way into her husband's home, kissed him, and let him touch my body. In fact, if his phone hadn't vibrated just then, I'm sure we'd have gone all the way.

"Akari, say you only found out the truth once the two of you were an item and you'd completely fallen for him. What do you think you'd have done? Would you have stayed together?"

I thought for a moment. What *would* I have done?

If I'd only learned later that he was married, would I have been too in love to break things off completely—no matter how unhappy the situation made me?

"No, I don't think so. No matter how much I liked him, as soon as I found out he was cheating, romance would have been out of the question."

Satsuki's expression became pained. "Because what—you hate the idea of an affair?"

"Yeah. Not just affairs. I can't stand dishonesty."

Hearing the decisive tone in my voice, Satsuki let out a chuckle.

"You really haven't changed, Akari."

"What do you mean?"

"Do you remember how, on the way to school, there was this pedestrian crossing that was always deserted? It was the kind where it was usually fine to cross even on a red light, and nobody really bothered to obey the signals. Apart from you, that is. When I was little, I used to watch you stubbornly obeying the red light and think, *Wow, she's so principled.*"

"When you were little? What about later?"

"I guess I still admired you for behaving so well, but began to realize that you were a bit of a stickler for the rules. . . ."

"I get that a lot."

A male voice interrupted our conversation. "Well, with Saturn in your first house, that's hardly a surprise. Being hard on yourself is in your nature."

We looked up and saw that the tuxedo cat had returned. He was carrying a tray on which a silver English teapot steamed, flanked by two porcelain cups.

"Saturn in my . . . first house?" I said, peering up at him. Satsuki looked as confused as I was.

"Oh yes," said the tuxedo cat solemnly. He set the cups down in front of us and poured some tea. "Mind if I read your stars quickly? The master's not here tonight, so I can't promise anything too complex . . ."

The cat produced something that looked like a

pocket watch from his apron, then pressed the winding crown inward.

There was a click. The face of the watch glowed. An instant later, a huge image of Saturn was projected onto the sky, right alongside the full moon.

I'd seen Saturn through the astronomical telescope at school before, but never this big. The large ring encircling the striped planet was mesmerizing.

"It's stunning . . ." murmured Satsuki, a delighted smile spreading across her lips.

The Persian cat reappeared and stood at our side with a tray of her own. "Yes, Saturn is a beautiful planet—but it's also very strict." She chuckled softly.

"Strict?" said Satsuki and I in unison, cocking our heads.

"V, I've told you before. I'd rather you didn't use that word about me," said the tuxedo cat, frowning as he folded his arms.

"Sorry," said the Persian, giving us a meaningful look. "But it's true, isn't it? In astrology, Saturn is known as the planet of trials."

" 'Trials' sounds a little . . . harsh," replied the tuxedo cat. "I prefer 'challenges,' personally."

The Persian gave an exasperated shrug. "You see, Saturn is sort of the schoolteacher in our lives."

"That I won't deny."

"Huh, *that* part's okay, is it?"

Watching this exchange between the cats, Satsuki and I could only blink in bafflement.

"My apologies," said the Persian. "In astrology, the house occupied by Saturn reveals the sorts of trials"—she bit her tongue, conscious of the tuxedo cat's glare—"sorry, *challenges* that an individual will face in life."

What were these challenges she was talking about?

"Here, this should make things a little easier to understand." The Persian took the pocket watch from the tuxedo cat, gave the winding crown a twist, then pressed it inward again.

The image of Saturn disappeared from the sky— and was replaced by a huge, clocklike diagram.

This must be a horoscope. There was a circle divided up into twelve segments, each labeled with a number. The numbers started on the left and cycled around in a counterclockwise direction.

MAI MOCHIZUKI

The tuxedo cat looked up at the diagram and frowned.

"*Self . . . money . . . knowledge . . .* don't you think you've oversimplified things slightly, V? I mean, take the third house. All it says is 'knowledge.' But it also stands for sibling relationships, not to mention communication. You *do* know that, don't you?"

"Oh yes," replied the Persian. "There are all sorts of deeper meanings. I just thought I'd keep things simple for now." Having dismissed the tuxedo cat's complaint, she turned to us. "The numbers refer to what we call 'houses.' For each of your houses, whether it aligns with a certain planet or constellation reveals all sorts about you. What you're good at and bad at, the type of people you're attracted to romantically, and the sorts of trials— ahem, *challenges*—you'll go through in life.

"For example, the first house always represents the self, but the position of the constellations relevant to it is what determines your general nature. If Aries is in your first house, you may be the hasty type; if it's Taurus, you'll be more easygoing—the complete opposite, in fact."

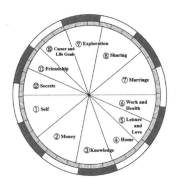

Satsuki looked quite confused by all this, but I'd taken an interest in astrology in the past—even reading a few books on the subject—and was just about able to grasp what they were talking about. The houses from one to twelve each had their own meanings. Depending on your date, time, and place of birth, the constellations and planets within them would vary.

"So if we want to know the biggest trials we'll face in life, we have to check which house Saturn is in . . ." I murmured, barely realizing I'd spoken aloud.

"That's right," said the Persian cat, clapping her paws together.

"*Challenges*, for goodness' sake," grumbled the tuxedo cat.

"For example," continued the Persian, "if Saturn is in your seventh house, which represents marriage, then you'll face . . . *challenges* in that area. Worrying about whether you'll ever find the one; your marriage hitting a bump in the road; dealing with a controlling partner—that sort of thing. You might wonder why your friends are all getting hitched and leading happy lives while your own journey to marital bliss is so arduous. But with Saturn in your seventh house, there's little use in fretting—that's just how it is."

People *did* seem to have wildly different experiences when it came to marriage. Some found their soulmate, received the blessing of both sets of parents, and got married in no time. For others, it was one stumbling block after another: first they struggled to meet anyone in the first place, then when they finally started dating someone they found it hard to make the leap to marriage. If they did persuade their partner to say yes, the parents would soon step in to oppose the match.

Even when a seemingly perfect couple tied the knot, their relationship could always hit the rocks later on. As the Persian cat had just pointed out, you might find yourself wedded to an overbearing partner, leading to endless anxiety and a diminishing sense of self-worth.

"So I have Saturn in that house, then?" asked Satsuki, her expression serious. But the tuxedo and the Persian cats shook their heads in unison.

"Actually, it's in your sixth house—the one that represents work and health," said the Persian.

At this, the sixth house in the horoscope in the sky suddenly began to glow.

"People with Saturn in their sixth house often land themselves incredibly demanding jobs. But their indomitable perseverance gets them through it—as does their highly professional approach to work. You didn't just succeed as an actor because you were drawn to the world of show business, but because you decided you were going to make a living out of it. You see, Satsuki, Saturn might be the planet of challenges—but if you face up to them, you can reap big rewards. But there's one other thing . . ."

"What's that?" asked Satsuki, leaning forward.

"The planet that governs love, beauty, interests, and hobbies is Venus," said the Persian, putting a hand to her chest as she went on. "With you, Satsuki, Venus is in your twelfth house, which represents secrets."

The twelfth house began to glow.

"People with Venus in this house are often drawn to some kind of clandestine romance, and face plenty of temptations in that regard. If they're not careful—well, it depends on the exact position of your stars, but it can end up making those Saturnian, work-related challenges a lot harder to deal with."

The tuxedo cat nodded, as if to say this was only natural.

Satsuki seemed deeply struck by their words.

"That makes sense. . . . See, it's not like I want to have an affair, but married men always seem to try their luck with me. And I do find myself drawn to them—they have that emotional stability in their life, that maturity that's often so lacking in single men. . . ."

"Married people can seem appealing precisely because they have a partner propping them up," interjected the tuxedo cat. "Their well-chosen clothes, their cleanliness, that emotional stability you mentioned—all that is only because they have someone to support them. No wonder you find them more appealing than your average singleton."

The cat's harsh words had reduced Satsuki to silence. Still, he wasn't wrong—and that was probably why married men lost a great deal of their charm as soon as they got divorced.

"I see," murmured Satsuki, biting her lip. "He might have been dazzling in my eyes, but I guess he only shone that way because his wife polished him up so much. And there I was, trying to snatch the fruit of all her labor."

For a moment, we simply sat there. Then, unable to bear the weight of the silence anymore, I opened my mouth.

"Does having Venus in your twelfth house always mean you end up having an affair?"

"Of course not," replied the Persian. "As I said, the twelfth house represents secrets—so yes, having Venus in there might mean having an affair, but it could also be a discreet office romance or an unspoken infatuation with a teacher. Or it might just mean you're drawn to stories featuring that sort of romance without ever embarking on one yourself."

"Right," I said with a nod. "And even if you do make a mistake, you can always mend your ways, earn people's trust again, and find happiness in love, can't you?"

"Oh yes," the tuxedo cat said with a nod. "Just remember the mirror principle and you'll be fine."

"The mirror principle?" I asked.

"Yes," said the Persian, revealing a mirror tucked inside the lid of the pocket watch. "You see, the stars aren't interested in policing things like infidelity or illicit love, or dishing out punishments. From their point of view, there's no such thing as right or wrong in the first place."

I furrowed my brow.

"Instead," continued the tuxedo cat with an expansive gesture, "our world is governed by the mirror principle. Everything you do in life is reflected back on you in time. Hurt someone, and it'll rebound on you eventually. Affairs inevitably cause a great deal of pain—especially when there's family involved. All that suffering will come back to haunt you."

Satsuki wrapped her arms around herself, frowning bitterly.

"So," she said weakly, "you're saying it's only natural that the world is treating me like this? I mean, it's not just his wife and kids I hurt—there are all his fans to think about, too . . ."

"Yes, there's that," said the Persian cat. "Plus the cosmos has a habit of making examples out of famous people."

"What does that mean?"

"For better or worse," cut in the tuxedo cat, "they're singled out as models for how we all behave. They become shining examples or cautionary tales: a paradigm of self-made success, or living proof of how a casual fling can ruin your life."

It was true: sometimes hearing about a famous person's transgression—be it an affair, illicit love, drugs—could help people see their own life a little more clearly. Telling themselves there was no way they'd let themselves be subjected to that level of outrage and risk losing everything, they'd resolve not to follow the celebrity's example.

"It's just as he says," said the Persian. "Satsuki, if you're planning on staying in show business, you'll have to remember that whatever you do is going to be put under the microscope." The cat's tone was gently admonishing.

"Do you think I should even try?" Satsuki's voice trembled slightly.

"That's for you to decide," replied the tuxedo cat bluntly, seeming not to notice that Satsuki was on the verge of tears.

"Hey, go easy on her," said the Persian, cuffing him around the head.

"I'm just telling her the truth. The stars don't decide your future. All they do is help you choose one for yourself."

It was as though two doors had appeared in front of Satsuki. One of them led away from the entertainment industry, onto a different path. The other led back to her life as an actor. Whichever she chose, it wouldn't be an easy ride. But for Satsuki right now,

the path back to acting looked particularly thorny—
and she seemed to recognize that.

"I . . ." she began, clenching her fists and looking
up. "I want to keep acting. Everyone hates me right
now. They can throw stones all they like—and they
will, I know. But I want to be an actress again. Even
if I have to claw my way back in."

The tuxedo cat nodded. "If that's your decision,
then all you have to do is stay true to the path you've
chosen."

I turned to the Persian cat.

"Satsuki's going through a bit of an ordeal at the
moment. Can astrology help her get back on her
feet?"

"Whenever we stumble in life, the most important thing is to really know ourselves—and I don't
just mean in the astrological sense," said the Persian
cat, raising one of her paws. "Think about it: When
you're trying to get somewhere and lose your way,
what do you do? You get out your map and check
which way you're supposed to be going. With Satsuki,
that means realizing that, more than other people,

she's susceptible to the lure of a secretive romance. But if she gives in to that temptation, she's bound to stop getting work. She has to realize that those two things are intertwined. And as a celebrity, people are going to want to make an example out of her. As long as she understands all that, she'll be ready to move on with her life."

"Satsuki," said the Persian, placing her soft paw on the actress's shoulder, "like I said before, Saturn is a harsh planet, one that likes to put us through our paces. But the challenges it sets us aren't barriers to confront—they're doors waiting to be opened."

The tuxedo cat nodded deeply.

A glimmer of hope had returned to Satsuki's eyes. "Doors . . . waiting to be opened?"

"That's right. If you can navigate the challenge, a new door will open for you—and the view from it will be a lot better. Saturn may be strict, but it richly rewards those who persevere." The Persian cat giggled. "You know, a bit like a schoolteacher—with mood swings."

The tuxedo cat cleared his throat loudly as if to silence his companion, then turned to Satsuki.

"Young lady, the path you've chosen won't be easy. Society will keep trying to put you on trial; nothing will change overnight. It will be a harsh journey indeed. But if you really are determined to be an actress, you'll just have to give it your all—in full awareness of what's in store."

"I'm in," said Satsuki in a firm voice, bowing her head in the tuxedo cat's direction. There was a steely strength in her gaze.

It seemed the tuxedo cat was . . . Saturn. In which case, did that mean the Persian cat was *actually* Venus?

"Now then, Akari."

I sat up instinctively, trembling all over. "Y-yes?"

"As Cronus here was just saying, you have Saturn in your first house—that of the self. That means you're diligent and motivated—but most of all, you're hard on yourself. Even when no one has a bad word to say about you, you're never happy with your achievements or yourself. Tell me, don't you find it a little hard to breathe sometimes?"

I did. In fact, right now, my throat felt tight.

"Let's have a look at your constellations," said the

tuxedo cat, folding his arms. "In your first house you have Leo, which is associated with a degree of flamboyance. You're likely to be drawn to the more glamorous things in life. Which is why you ended up choosing a job in the media."

The Persian cat clapped her paws together. "Now then, you two. We've got some desserts lined up for you. First, Satsuki," she said, setting a large glass down on the table. Next she produced a cooler bag, from which she extracted two spheres of yellow ice cream and placed them into the glass. They seemed to have been sprinkled with some kind of gold dust, and twinkled in the moonlight like a miniature constellation.

"This is Venus Ice Cream—unparalleled in its sweetness," said the Persian cat.

Next, the tuxedo cat brought over a glass coffeepot. "And if I pour this Moonlight Coffee, our house specialty, over it, the result"—he began pouring the coffee over the ice cream, causing it to melt irresistibly—"is a Planetary Affogato." He moved the glass toward Satsuki.

Satsuki tried a spoonful of the affogato. "Wow . . ."

she murmured eventually. "The ice cream is so sweet, but the slight bitterness of the coffee balances it out perfectly. What a combination!"

Maybe the Planetary Affogato was a kind of message from the two cats. Satsuki couldn't just give in to the sweetness of temptation—she had to remember the bitter consequences, too.

"And Akari, this is for you," said the Persian cat.

I turned and gasped with delight. On a white plate, topped with a ball of vanilla ice cream, was a devilish-looking chocolate dessert.

"This is a Lunar Chocolate Fondant, with a rich chocolate sauce . . ." The Persian began pouring the sauce. The mere sight of the fondant made me salivate. "There you go," she said, smiling as she set the dessert in front of me.

"It looks delicious," I said, bowing my head as I reached slowly for my spoon. As I inserted it into the cake, a river of thick molten chocolate came oozing out.

My eyes widened with anticipation as I brought a spoonful of fondant to my lips. The flavor was even richer than I'd expected, the freezing ice cream smoothly giving way to the velvety sweetness of the chocolate sauce.

"It's incredible. Really—incredible." It was so delicious that I could only repeat the word "incredible." When had I last treated myself to something like this?

Watching me, the tuxedo cat allowed himself a smile.

"The full moon also has the power of liberation, you know."

"Liberation?"

"Akari, it's wonderful that you always strive so hard to do the right thing," said the tuxedo cat in a gentle tone. "But that's not all there is to life. Sometimes, you have to know how to go easy on yourself."

At these words, something deep inside me finally gave way.

I'd never stopped blaming myself for getting involved with a married man. Friends would tell me it wasn't my fault and that I didn't know. But I had *sensed* that he might be involved with another woman—so why hadn't I asked him about it? Just because I was in the dark, it didn't mean I was completely blameless in the matter, did it? And so I carried on beating myself up about it. Even now, half a year later, I still wasn't ready to let myself off the hook.

It wasn't just the affair, either. Ever since I was a little girl, I'd been unable to bear the idea of failure, of being in the wrong.

"You sure you're okay, Cro? You're not normally this nice to people. . . ." The Persian cat giggled.

The tuxedo frowned. " 'Cro . . .'?"

Ignoring Cronus's apparent discomfort with this nickname, the Persian turned back to me. "It's just like he says: forgiving yourself is important, Akari. It's not just that you're too hard on yourself—you sometimes end up projecting that harshness onto others, too. Don't you think that's a little unfair?"

I felt stung by her words. It was true: it wasn't just myself I held to absurd standards, but also those around me. Not to mention my tendency to feel mad at anyone who could effortlessly achieve things I found impossible—though deep down that was pure envy . . .

"Sometimes, if you want to be compassionate toward others, you have to be kind to yourself first. If you obsess too much over the restrictions you've placed on yourself, you'll lose sight of what you really want. Instead, liberate yourself. Embrace who you really are."

If I was too hard on myself all the time, it would only lead to periodic explosions of emotion. And after each explosion, I'd fall into a negative cycle of blaming myself. Looking after myself, while being big-hearted enough to accept myself and others for who they were—that sounded like a better way for me to live. But there was one thing I didn't quite get. What part of me in particular needed freeing? Who, or what, was I supposed to accept?

Seeing me frown, the Persian cat propped her chin on one paw. "Come on, Akari, let's be honest. You're in love!"

"What?" I replied, my eyes practically retreating into their sockets. "Me? Oh no. No, Takumi is ancient history as far as I'm concerned."

The moment I'd discovered he was married, and

that he'd been hiding that from me the whole time, every drop of attraction I'd felt for him had evaporated. By now, I didn't feel a thing for him.

"Do you think you can hide your secrets from me?" said the Persian cat, leveling her golden eyes at me. It was as though she was peering right into the depths of my soul. Unable to hold her gaze, I turned to one side.

"The person you love isn't exactly the type you'd normally go for—which is why you're struggling to recognize your feelings, isn't it?"

My shoulders trembled involuntarily.

"Saturn might want your partner to be some highflier whom everyone will admire," continued the Persian. "But the person you've actually fallen for is a slightly different proposition. And so you're deceiving yourself. Akari—it's no use running away from the truth!"

Finally, the image of a certain man flitted across my mind.

Akari, darling . . .

There he was.

Jiro.

"No, it can't be . . . See, the thing is, he's too——"

Too what? Before I could finish, the Persian cat stopped me with a sharp glance.

Yes, I'd long admired Jiro's enthusiasm for his job, and how popular he was with everyone——not to mention that piercing insight of his. But because I'd convinced myself he was gay, I'd told myself I didn't feel anything for him. In fact, I'd done such a good job of ignoring my emotions that I'd begun to feel positively uncomfortable around him.

"You mean even if the person in question isn't attracted to me at all?"

The chances of Jiro being into women seemed remote. So even if I did have feelings for him, they would never lead to anything.

The Persian cat gave a quick nod. "Remember what I said just now? Whenever you feel lost, stop for a moment. Get your bearings. You need to take a look at yourself, and accept what you see, before you can take a single step forward."

I understood. Before I even started worrying about

whether Jiro could reciprocate my feelings, the important thing was to recognize those feelings—and accept them.

Yes, I'm in love with him.

The moment I admitted this to myself, my chest felt as if it had caught fire. Tears welled in my eyes and burned their way down my cheeks. I wasn't just crying about the Jiro thing. It was everything up until now. Throughout my life, I'd always been my harshest critic, constantly policing my own desires. As a kid, I'd wanted to buy sweets on the way home from school, just like my friends. I'd wanted to dye my hair during the summer. I'd even wanted to get piercings. But because these things were considered "bad," I could never admit that they appealed to me. Instead, I not only denied myself these pleasures, but also looked down upon anyone who didn't.

At one point, I'd had a crush on a boy with a rebellious streak. But I'd smothered my feelings for him and tricked myself into thinking I only liked guys who were on the straight and narrow. I'd constantly tried to be someone who "always did the right

137

thing"—and only spent time with people who would confirm me in that belief.

Love had never really entered the equation. It was about always prioritizing what seemed "right." My actual feelings had been left to roam in the cold.

Now, finally, I could embrace who I really was. I felt a thrill of inner joy.

"Of course, it's wonderful that you've always been so well-behaved," said the tuxedo cat. "But life is like one of those black-and-white spinning tops that turns into a beautiful whirl of color once it spins fast enough. It's all about keeping things in balance."

The Persian nodded emphatically. "Even a washing machine won't spin right if it's not level."

"Really, V?" said the tuxedo cat. "Where did you get *that* metaphor from?"

"I just thought it might help her understand!"

Watching them bicker, Satsuki and I exchanged a grin.

"Well, enjoy your food," said the Persian.

The cats withdrew in the direction of the café. We bowed our heads and carried on savoring our desserts.

THE FULL MOON COFFEE SHOP

Their elegant flavors were like a balm for body and mind.

When I'd finished, I sighed and glanced over at Satsuki, who was gazing up at the night sky. She looked content, as if she, too, had finally found some kind of peace.

As for the expression on my face—I imagine it looked a lot like hers.

I had learned to know and accept myself. And with a little help from the dessert, that tightness at the back of my throat seemed to have vanished— along with the heaviness in my heart.

I felt overwhelmed with gratitude toward the cats.

I turned around, murmuring the words, "Thank you"—only to find that the Full Moon Coffee Shop had vanished.

"What the . . . ?" I blurted, my eyes widening in surprise. Until a moment ago, we'd been sitting on the chairs outside the café, but now we found our-selves back on the park bench. "No way!"

This was getting too wild.

Satsuki chuckled at my side. "Maybe we were be-witched by tanuki."

"Tanuki? You're trying to say those weren't cats but raccoon dogs?" I asked, recalling the tuxedo cat's sullen expression.

Satsuki fell silent—and then I caught her eye, and we both burst out laughing.

"Uh-oh," said Satsuki, grimacing as she got her phone out. "Look at all these missed calls from my manager . . ."

"I guess we should head home . . ." I said, getting to my feet.

"Yeah, we probably should," replied Satsuki, and we began to walk. "You know, Akari, I think I'm going to write a letter of apology to his wife and kids. I was so upset when my own dad cheated—and yet I've ended up following in his footsteps. I feel terrible. I doubt they'll forgive me, but I still want to say sorry."

I nodded in silent response.

"Then I want to hold a press conference," she went on. There was fresh conviction in her eyes. "See, I've finally understood something. If the world is angry with me, it's because so many people were hurt by what I did. Every single person I come across could be someone I've upset. That seems like something worth apologizing for. I'm sure it'll be a while before I have any work, but when something does come my way, I swear I'll pour my heart and soul into it—whatever it is."

"I know you will," I said, nodding. "I'll be rooting for you, Satsuki."

"I'll be rooting for you, too, Akari." She abruptly leaned toward me. "By the way . . . who's the guy?"

I practically choked. "That's . . . a secret for now."

"If you insist," said Satsuki with a shrug. "Still, there is something I wanted to ask you." Her face had taken on a slightly pained expression.

What could she want? I wondered. Was she going to ask me to put in a good word for her with a producer I knew?

But in the end, her request turned out to be something quite unexpected. When she spoke, it was in a shy voice, her eyes glued to the ground.

"Do you think maybe, sometime, we could go out for cake together again?"

In an instant, the taste of those exquisite desserts came rushing back to me.

"Oh, of course!" I nodded enthusiastically.

Satsuki beamed back at me.

And *that* is the story of the strange moonlit night on which I learned to know myself—and finally move forward with my life.

CHAPTER 3

A RETROGRADE REUNION

PART ONE: MERCURY CREAM SODA

TAKASHI MIZUMOTO

1

Here we go again, thought Takashi Mizumoto. Sitting in front of his computer, he tutted loudly and put his head in his hands.

Yuichi Yasuda, his old university friend and fellow

entrepreneur, was peering over his shoulder at the screen. "What's up?"

"Data's partially corrupted," said Takashi, leaning back in his chair and letting out a long sigh.

"Uh-oh," replied Yuichi, turning slightly pale. "Are we in trouble?"

Takashi smiled wryly. "Nah, we'll be fine. I mean, I do have a backup . . ."

"Phew. Don't scare me like that, okay?"

"Yeah, but . . ."—*but it'll still be a pain to fix*, he wanted to add. But his partner already knew that. Takashi sipped his coffee silently.

They were sitting in their one-room office in Osaka, not far from Umeda Station. Being based in Umeda, the business district, made their start-up sound like a pretty big deal, but in reality the office barely measured thirty square yards.

He and Yuichi were the joint executives and sole employees of the small IT venture they'd started together. Its name was formed from the first letters of their last names: M Y Systems. People had a habit of mispronouncing it "My Systems."

Wow, you manage an IT company? Amazing. So . . . what exactly do you do?

People would ask some variation on these questions whenever they were out drinking. It had come up just the other day, when Takashi had bumped into a woman he'd been at primary school with. The fact that he worked in IT seemed to impress people and yet at the same time they usually had no idea what the job entailed.

Takashi was mainly a server security engineer. He set up, built, operated, and maintained the servers for company websites. His partner, Yuichi, was more involved with the creative side. He designed websites for companies, and recently had been experimenting with building mobile dating games.

They'd known each other since university. One day, Yuichi had turned to him and said, "If we're going to start a company, don't you think we should do it while we're still students with nothing to lose?" It had made such an impression on Takashi that he'd agreed on the spot—and that was how M Y Systems was born.

They were students—what was the worst that could happen?

Maybe this recklessness was the key to their success. In any case, the company had gotten off to a pretty smooth start and by now boasted decent profits.

At first they'd worked from home, but as freelancers the taxes were nothing to sniff at and they'd found it hard to separate work from their private lives. So they'd decided to lease an office in Umeda. It wasn't big, but it was enough for the two of them.

"Crap. Looks like I'm going to have to re-input the data."

"My condolences," said Yuichi, making a prayer sign with his hands. He was evidently amused by Takashi's plight.

Yuichi's cheerful, outgoing personality hadn't changed since their university days. In fact, even though it was five years since their graduation, people often assumed he was a student. Guys like him were pretty common in the IT world. Takashi, on the other hand, was the quiet type—in fact, he was basically Yuichi's polar opposite. When he was a student, people had often assumed he was an office worker.

As a small business, they spent a lot of their time pitching their services to other companies. The youthful, flashily dressed Yuichi could make clients uncomfortable, while Takashi's calm demeanor seemed to put their minds at ease.

All in all, thought Takashi, they made a pretty decent pair.

"I know data loss is an occupational hazard for us," said Yuichi, putting his hands on his hips, "but I feel like this happens to you more than the average person."

"Tell me about it," said Takashi with another deep sigh. He'd noticed, too: for some reason, bugs like this seemed to be the bane of his existence.

It was always the same, he thought. Once the trouble started, it wasn't just data that would get corrupted. Emails from regular clients would suddenly end up in his spam folder for no discernible reason. Even trains and planes seemed to suffer more delays when he was on board.

Which reminds me. I should check my spam folder.

He reached for his mouse, already sick with worry.

He opened the folder and immediately clapped a hand to his forehead. "Not again . . ."

"What is it this time?"

"An email from someone I know ended up in my spam."

"Oh. A work contact?"

"No, a friend. Actually, we were at primary school together . . ." Takashi's voice trailed off.

"Ah," said Yuichi, turning to him with an excited glint in his eye. "The one who works at that famous hair salon in Umeda?"

"Did I tell you about her?"

He thought back to the day he'd bumped into her. He'd been in an uncharacteristically good mood afterward, and had excitedly told Yuichi the whole story as soon as he got back to the office.

●　　●　　●

About two months before, he'd gone out to buy a sandwich for lunch. A woman in the bakery had turned to him and asked, "Are you Takashi, by any chance? Takashi Mizumoto? With the dad who ran a construction firm . . . ?"

Her warm smile and gentle demeanor had appealed to him straightaway. But, struggling to place her, he'd inadvertently frowned.

"Sorry," she'd said, "I must have gotten you mixed up with someone."

"No, I . . ." Takashi blurted. "That's me, Takashi, and my dad was in construction. But who are . . ."

Her small round eyes widened slightly. Then she chuckled. "Right, of course you don't recognize me . . . Megumi Hayakawa."

Even with her name, Takashi struggled to place her. She explained that they'd been at primary school together. He'd guessed they were the same age, but she turned out to be three years his senior. She only knew him because they'd been in the same walk-to-school group—so maybe it wasn't too surprising that he hadn't remembered her. In fact, if anything was surprising, it was that she remembered him.

"Of course I remember you," she said. "You made

quite an impression on me, you see . . . I was always grateful for what you did back then."

She smiled at him. He gave a vague, slightly nonplussed bow in return. He had a feeling he knew what she was referring to—but he didn't remember doing anything that would merit *this* level of gratitude.

Before he left the bakery, she'd explained that she worked at a nearby hairdressing salon, on a street he often walked down. From that day on, they began bumping into each other from time to time.

When she saw him through the window, she'd smile and wave. Takashi's face would turn blank as he tried to hide his embarrassment. Just returning her bow was enough to get his pulse racing.

The salon took male customers, and he'd been thinking about getting his own hair cut there. The problem was, he hadn't seen her for a while. Maybe her shifts had changed, or maybe it was just coincidence that they hadn't run into each other. Secretly, he worried that she might have fallen ill.

Now she'd sent an email to his work address. Actually, she'd sent it two days ago—but because it had gone into his spam folder, he'd only just noticed it.

The email began:

Dear Mr. Takashi Mizumoto of M Y Systems, this is Megumi Hayakawa, your old primary-school acquaintance. I didn't know how else to contact you, so I've taken the liberty of writing to your work address.

It was true that they hadn't exchanged contact details. She must have found his address by searching online for his company.

I recently stopped working at the salon in Umeda for personal reasons. For now, I've taken up at my parents' beauty parlor instead. I say "for now" because actually I've realized I want to take my life in a slightly different direction. I'm thinking of making my own website, and wondered if I could talk to you about it?

Reading the email, Takashi's heart began hammering against his chest.

"So, what's the hairdresser say?" asked Yuichi from behind his back.

Takashi's shoulders quivered slightly. Designing

151

websites was Yuichi's job, not his. But if it was just for an individual, rather than a company, he could definitely put something together. He glanced back at the screen.

In the end, all he said was "She's quit that Umeda salon."

Yuichi's attention seemed to already have wandered elsewhere. "Oh yeah?" he murmured, staring at his own computer screen.

Relieved by this apparent lack of interest, Takashi began typing out his reply.

Sure, whenever you like. Just let me know where would be good to meet.

After reading his bland-sounding email to himself several times, he pressed the send button.

Just as it zipped out of his outbox, Yuichi let out an audible gasp.

Takashi looked up and frowned. "What's up?"

"Just listen to this," said Yuichi, leaning forward. "You know that mobile game I've been working on?"

He held his phone up. On it, Takashi could see various illustrations of handsome male characters, all lined up in a row. It was the dating game for women that Yuichi had been creating—although, technically, he was only handling the design and programming. The script itself was outsourced to writers.

"So it's been getting a bit of buzz recently. People seem to love the ending of one of the side characters."

"Right," said Takashi. He had heard about it, actually. In this game, you had to select the character who would be the object of your affection. Bagging one of the high-difficulty characters gave people the biggest sense of achievement. But players who found that too much of a challenge—or who just wanted to try something different—would deliberately try to seduce one of the side characters instead.

Recently, a storyline for one particular side character had been generating a lot of hype online. The character in question wasn't very handsome compared to some of the heroes—nor was he particularly wealthy. There weren't even any particularly steamy love scenes in his storyline. But despite his limitations, he really knew how to turn on the charm. When you got to his ending, he'd take the player's hand and say, "You're a princess in my eyes—and just being with you has been enough to make me feel like a prince. Thank you for a truly wonderful time." Then he'd kiss the back of her hand. And that was how the storyline ended.

Social media was awash with excited reactions to the story, and in particular the character's gallant behavior. Soon, players were clamoring for a sequel to the romance or the addition of racier love scenes, with some even saying they'd be happy to pay for additional content.

"It was Serika who did the script for that character, right?" asked Takashi.

Yuichi might have developed the game, but it had still been released under the company's name and Takashi had familiarized himself with all the details.

"Yeah," said Yuichi. "So, are you ready for the surprising part? Seriously," he added, holding up a palm, "I hope you can handle this."

With this sort of a buildup, Takashi thought, it was going to be pretty hard to be surprised by anything.

"Well, as the story has been such a hit, I asked the

scriptwriter to do us a sequel. She was over the moon . . . I mean, I guess any scriptwriter would be pleased to see their story going down so well."

"Sure." Takashi nodded.

"And now this article appears," said Yuichi, waving his phone screen in Takashi's direction again.

Fans have been going wild for the charming side character in a dating game. Its anonymous writer, who provided the script under the pen name Serika, turns out to be none other than Mizuki Serikawa!

"*What!*" Takashi snatched Yuichi's phone.

"See. Told you it was a surprise. Turns out we outsourced our story to *the* Mizuki Serikawa!"

"Wow," said Takashi as he scanned the article. The author had approached Serika for an interview about the script that had gone viral. She'd accepted— before going on to reveal her real identity.

In her comments, she'd explained that she wanted players to be able to enjoy the side character endings as much as the main characters' and was, of course, delighted at the storyline's success.

"I knew you'd be surprised, but you've really exceeded my expectations," Yuichi said with a grin. He held his hand out. "Can I have my phone back now?"

Takashi wordlessly returned the phone. But what had shocked him so much was the name, *Mizuki Serikawa*. If it had been anyone else, no matter how renowned a scriptwriter, he wouldn't have been this astonished. But it was Miss Serikawa, of all people . . .

As he sat there, his shoulders hunched together in surprise, his phone chimed to let him know he had an email on his work account.

It was from Megumi Hayakawa.

Thank you very much. How about next Monday? My parents' beauty parlor is closed on Mondays, so we could meet there, if you don't mind the trip?

Takashi's face creased into a smile. He started tapping out his reply right away.

2

It was the following Monday—the day of his meeting with Megumi Hayakawa.

Again? Seriously? How was he this late?

As he finally boarded his train, Takashi was brimming with frustration and impatience. They'd arranged to meet in the early evening. He'd worked from home that day and had set an alarm to tell him when to leave before busying himself with his work. Or at least that's what he'd *thought* he'd done—but for some reason his alarm had failed to go off and now he was way behind schedule.

He'd rushed about getting ready, then dashed to the station—only to find that the train, which was almost never late, had been delayed due to a thunderstorm. When he finally climbed on board, he collapsed into his seat. It looked as if he'd just about make it on time.

The sky was still a bright blue. Could there really have been a storm on a day like this?

The beauty parlor run by Megumi's parents was in the Otesuji shopping arcade in Fushimi. Takashi lived in the Yodoyabashi neighborhood of Osaka, which meant it was a single ride all the way to Fushimi-Momoyama, the nearest station to the beauty parlor.

Takashi got his phone out and glared at it reproachfully. On closer inspection, it seemed he'd merely selected the time without actually activating the alarm. He couldn't quite believe he was capable of a mistake like that.

Data corruption, emails going missing, trains running late . . . There were times in his life when everything seemed to go wrong at once.

Takashi accessed the company's social media account.

It looked as if Mizuki Serikawa was trending.

Can't believe it was THE Mizuki Serikawa who did that script!

Makes sense, though. I mean, it was so good . . .

Absolutely dying to see the sequel!

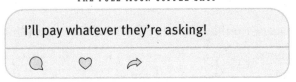

I'll pay whatever they're asking!

Among these excited reactions, there was a mercifully small number of more negative comments. One of them read: "So a former 'hitmaker' ends up changing her name and writing storylines for side characters in a game? Talk about hitting rock bottom . . ."

First Megumi Hayakawa, and now Mizuki Serikawa—life really was coming full circle . . .

He might not have remembered Megumi, but Miss Serikawa was vivid in his memory. All these encounters with people from the past seemed to be coinciding with his recent spate of technical woes. *How very weird*, he thought.

When he was about twenty minutes away from his destination, the train came to an unexpected halt at one of the stations along the way.

"As a result of the earlier thunderstorm, another train is experiencing electrical difficulties. Our apologies for the delay. We'll get moving again as soon as possible."

More trouble? thought Takashi, putting a hand to his brow.

Feeling a fresh wave of frustration and impatience, he dashed off a text message to Megumi, explaining that he'd be late because of the train.

Her reply came quickly.

> Okay—don't worry, take your time!

His shoulders sagged with relief.

The train didn't seem to be going anywhere soon. He was beginning to feel a little sleepy. The night before, he'd been so nervous about seeing Megumi he'd barely slept.

He folded his arms as his eyelids began to droop.

I'll just have a brief nap.

But it wasn't long until he sank into a deep sleep.

In his dream, someone was patting him on the shoulder and saying, "Hey, come on, we're almost there!"

The next station is Fushimi-Momoyama.

His eyes snapped open as the onboard announcement reached his ears. It looked as if the train had started moving again. They were almost there!

Phew—almost slept past my stop . . .

The train was still moving, but Takashi scrambled to his feet, pinching his brow in an effort to wake himself up. He wasn't sure how deeply he'd slept, but he knew he'd had an incredibly vivid dream.

3

The train pulled in at Fushimi-Momoyama Station and Takashi hopped off. The journey that should have taken him just under an hour had ended up taking almost ninety minutes. Still, he felt a lot better after his sleep—in fact, he was a new man.

He'd already told Megumi he'd be late, so he was in no rush as he left the station.

I remember hearing something about the entrance to the Otesuji shopping arcade being a little unusual, he thought. He decided he might take a look. A short way from the entrance, he stopped to take in the scenery.

The railway ran right past the shopping arcade,

and its entrance was guarded by a level crossing whose barriers lowered every time a train went by. It was a curious sight—one that filled him with a sort of childlike awe.

Turning around so that he faced directly away from the arcade, he could just make out the grand torii gate of the historic Gokonomiya Shrine, looming at the far end of the shop-lined street.

It's actually pretty nice around here.

Takashi's parents hailed from downtown Kyoto, where they'd run a small construction firm. Now, though, they'd retired and moved out to the country. But when his parents still lived in the heart of the city, neither they nor he had seen much of the outside world. Citizens of central Kyoto were known for insisting that the Fushimi neighborhood wasn't *really* Kyoto—a claim never made entirely in jest.

But now, with a bit more perspective on the city, Takashi could see that downtown Kyoto and places like Fushimi on its outskirts each had their own appeal. Above the entrance to the arcade was a sign bearing a large OTE logo, and below, the full name: OTESUJI. He made his way into the arcade, where he was greeted by exactly the kind of nostalgic scene he'd hoped to encounter.

The arcade was lined with old-fashioned coffee shops as well as stylish modern cafés. Takashi sighed with delight at the lively, bustling atmosphere. Candy shops, bakeries, izakaya bars, small supermarkets, pharmacies: the arcade seemed to have everything you could ever want in one place.

Between the shops, he spotted a red gate emblazoned with the words DAIKOJI TEMPLE. Almost without thinking, he reached for his phone and looked it up online. It was dedicated to three deities: the Buddha of Limitless Light, the Buddha of Healing, and Jizo, the guardian deity of travelers and children. It had been associated with the Fushimi-no-miya branch of the imperial family and founded almost eight hundred years ago. A temple located slap-bang in the middle of a shopping arcade, which "just happened" to have a rich and illustrious history—that was *very* Kyoto.

Farther down the arcade, he spotted a sky-blue sign: AQUA BEAUTY PARLOR. Just as Megumi had told him, the notice on the door read CLOSED ON MONDAYS.

With a nervous quiver, he knocked on the door.

"Hi!" came Megumi's voice. "Come on in."

"Hi," he said, bowing slightly as he walked in.

He found himself in a typical old-school beauty parlor. Megumi smiled at him. She was wearing a black waist apron, almost as if he had caught her in the middle of work.

Just as he was about to return her smile, his expression froze.

There was a customer sitting in one of the chairs. A woman, probably around thirty, who was glancing slightly nervously in the mirror.

"Sorry, Takashi, do you mind waiting on the sofa while I finish up here?" Megumi waved a hand apologetically, then returned to her position behind the customer.

Takashi nodded and sat down on the sofa in the waiting area.

Megumi sprayed mist onto the customer's hair, then combed it thoroughly. With impressive dexterity, she braided the hair, then carefully styled it.

"There we go. All done!" she said, patting her customer on the shoulder.

"Thanks, Meg. Wow—who'd have thought just getting my hair styled would make such a difference!"

So they're friends, then, thought Takashi.

"Well, they do say that hair makes all the difference . . ." replied Megumi, holding up an index finger.

"Do they?" said the woman.

"Just taking a little care over our hair can make us feel brand-new—that applies to women, men, even animals." Megumi reached for a small comb. "Especially when you factor in eyebrows and eyelashes." She ran the comb through the woman's eyebrows, then switched to an eyelash curler and gave her lashes a lift.

The friend looked in the mirror and smiled at this dazzling new version of herself.

"Thank you *so* much."

"Not at all—thanks for telling me about that job!"

"Seriously, you'll be doing me a favor. Jiro will be delighted. I mean, as hairdressers go, you're pretty first-rate."

"I'm honored. Tell Jiro I'm looking forward to working with him!"

"I will."

"You're meeting him this evening, right?" said Megumi, removing the cape from around her friend's neck. "Akari, you're going to blow him away looking like this."

"Ah—let's hope so . . ." the woman murmured awkwardly as she got up from the chair.

"Well, see you soon!"

"Yeah. Let's go for dinner sometime."

"Absolutely."

Megumi saw her friend out of the shop with a smile, then turned to Takashi.

"Thanks for coming all this way, and sorry for the wait. You said you'd be a little late, so I thought I'd do my friend's hair before her date. She actually popped by to tell me about a job opportunity."

"Not at all. Sorry I took so long."

Megumi shook her head as if to say he didn't need to apologize. "Fancy a coffee?"

"Please."

"Hot or iced?"

"Iced, please." He was pretty thirsty, he realized, loosening his tie slightly in an attempt to calm his nerves. He was technically here on business, and he'd made sure to dress the part. If he was honest, though, that wasn't entirely true. He had such little confidence in his dress sense that a suit had seemed the safest option.

Megumi wasn't beautiful in the conventional sense, nor was she really his usual type. And yet from the day they'd met, he'd felt intensely attracted to her. As for why, he couldn't exactly explain.

Soon Megumi reappeared with a glass of iced coffee on a tray. The freshly poured milk was still swirling around, gradually permeating the dark black coffee.

"I added a bit of milk and syrup—is that okay? If you prefer it black, I can have this one."

"No, that's fine. I take hot coffee black, but this is just how I like it when it's iced."

"Actually, this is a Sunrise Syrup coffee."

"A sunrise what?" asked Takashi, blinking.

She chuckled mischievously. "I had this amazing dream a while ago. I was served a drink called a Sunrise Syrup Iced Coffee, and it was so delicious I've been trying to re-create it. Haven't had much luck, though . . ."

As she spoke, Takashi took a sip and felt a refreshing sweetness spread through him.

"Weird, isn't it," she went on. "Remembering the taste of an iced coffee from a dream."

"Actually, I had a dream on the way here. I dozed off on the train. I can't remember exactly what the dream was, but I felt like someone was serving *me* a delicious drink, too."

She bent down toward him, leaning in so that her body almost formed a right angle. "Wow. What else?"

Takashi trembled ever so slightly. "That's the thing—I don't quite remember . . ."

What *had* happened in his dream?

4

In the dream, just like in reality, I was riding a train.

From somewhere came the strains of Beethoven's *Pastoral* Symphony. The train was chugging through an appropriately rural landscape, fields and rice paddies on either side.

What am I doing out here in the sticks?

My head was too unfocused to worry about that for long. The light outside was almost blinding.

I must be dreaming.

The train's gentle jolting felt pleasant, as if I was being rocked in a cradle. The train slowly chugged its way through the lush green countryside, until eventually it came to a halt in the middle of a field.

The people on the train began excitedly disembarking. I slowly got to my feet, too, and made my way off the train.

Looking around, I could make out a mountain on the other side of the expanse of fields.

I've seen this landscape before.

Then it came to me. This place looked a lot like the area my parents now lived in—Miyama, in the district of Nantan.

When I was in primary school, I'd visited this area with my parents. Gazing out across the peaceful landscape, they'd said, "When we retire, we want to move somewhere like this. Take it nice and easy."

A fresh breeze caressed my cheeks. Above the verdant fields, the setting sun was slowly burning the sky crimson. The moon was out and full.

At the end of a road, I spotted what looked like a pop-up café.

In front of a small truck were several sets of wooden tables and chairs, where the passengers from the train were sitting. I recognized them, somehow, and yet their faces remained a blur.

I took a seat at a free two-seater table. Someone appeared and placed a glass in front of me. "Here you go. A Mercury Cream Soda."

Unlike the scenery and people around me, the drink was vivid and distinct. It had all the usual components of a cream soda—ice cream and a cherry perched on top. What distinguished it from the normal version was that its soda wasn't the usual green, but instead a beautiful sky blue, and the ice cream was a grayish-white color rather than the usual vanilla.

I pulled the glass toward me and sipped the drink through the straw.

The soda tasted pleasant and refreshing as it trickled down my throat, and the sweetness was just right. The taste was vaguely familiar and yet totally new.

The pale gray ice cream turned out to be a lemon-flavored sorbet that went perfectly with the soda. As the flavors danced on my palate, I caught the sound of a woman's voice from the neighboring table. She seemed to be complaining about something.

"Emails getting lost, data corrupting itself, and now the train's late . . . Sheesh!"

The woman could have taken the words right out of my own mouth. It was as if she was giving voice to my inner thoughts.

"Typical Mercury retrograde, isn't it?" she continued.

I couldn't help turning to look. When I did, however, I found not a woman but a cat. A cat with fluffy white fur. Probably a Persian or a Chinchilla, I thought.

And the cat was . . . talking?

"Come on, V, don't make it sound like it's my fault," came a voice from across the table, where another cat sat. This one was a Siamese, with piercing light blue eyes and a boyish voice.

"Oh, I'm not saying it's your fault, M."

"Who's M? My name's Mercury, I think you'll find."

"You're the one who keeps calling me V when my name is Venus."

Though the people around me were still only vague

outlines, the cats were entirely distinct. Even for a dream, it was pretty surreal.

And what was that about a "Mercury retrograde"?

After a moment, Venus turned to me and waved a paw. I bowed awkwardly in return, then took another sip of my cream soda.

The taste really was familiar.

"Pretty retro, don't you think?" said Venus. "The Mercury Cream Soda. Perfect for a Mercury retrograde. Great choice by the master."

"Oh, definitely," Mercury said with a nod in response.

The two cats were both looking at my drink. I decided to say something.

"Umm . . ." I began nervously. "I've actually been having just the kind of problems you mentioned just now. What was it that you said about a Mercury retrograde?"

This *was* a dream, after all. I might as well be upfront. If I'd been awake, I probably wouldn't have dared.

"Ah," said Mercury, narrowing his sky-blue eyes. "Well, a Mercury retrograde means Mercury is . . . in retrograde."

"Seriously, M?" said Venus, pouting at this somewhat simplistic explanation. "That doesn't exactly help him, does it? Now, I'm sure you're familiar with the planet Mercury. Well, around three times a year, there's a period where it moves backward—in other words, when it's in retrograde."

"It goes backward?" I said, cocking my head slightly. "Do the planets . . . do that?"

"Ah—it doesn't actually go backward," cut in Mercury. "It's just that, from the Earth, during that period, it *appears* to be doing so. A sort of optical illusion, if you like."

"An optical illusion?" I said, folding my arms. "Huh . . ."

"Because Mercury orbits closer to the Sun than any of the other planets in the solar system and travels at a different speed from the Earth, it sometimes looks as though it's moving backward. You know how sometimes when you're on a train, or the highway, and the car or train next to you seems to go backward, even though you're actually traveling in the same direction? It's a bit like that."

"Right . . . And that happens three times a year?"

"Yes. For about three weeks each time."

That seemed like a pretty long time.

"Quite a while, isn't it?" said Venus, as if reading my mind. "Mercury governs the airwaves and communications. But when it appears to be traveling backward, the planet's power is reversed, too. During the retrograde, electrical and communication devices tend to undergo all sorts of malfunctions. Emails might not arrive, or trains and planes might be delayed."

Now that I thought about it, my periods of trouble with data or electronics always seemed to last for around a month. I'd be tearing my hair out and then one day the problems would stop as suddenly as they'd started, and life would go back to normal.

"Right—so those periods of trouble are because Mercury is in retrograde," I said, somewhat convinced. "But," I asked, frowning, "why does my colleague Yuichi never seem to have any problems?"

While I was dealing with all sorts of trouble—lost data, late-running trains—Yuichi always seemed to emerge completely unscathed.

"Well, some people are more vulnerable to the effects of the retrograde than others," replied Mercury casually.

"It depends on the position of your stars and the period in question—in your case, you have Mercury in your sixth house, which would explain why you feel the effects so strongly. But it brings blessings as well as downsides."

"Mercury in my . . . sixth house? What does that mean?"

"He's talking astrology," answered Venus. "The sixth house symbolizes work and health. And in your case, it has Mercury in it. Which explains why you're so suited to working in IT—it's all about data and communication, isn't it? However, at the same time, that makes you more vulnerable to Mercury's effects."

So I had Mercury in my sixth house, which related to work. That meant I received more of a blessing from Mercury than other people—but also that I was more susceptible to the planet's effects. In that case, instead of plugging away at work during the retrograde, maybe I should see it as a chance for some time off. I took a deep breath, looking around at the fields on all sides. I could visit my parents' home, I thought. I was overdue a visit.

Then something occurred to me. I looked worriedly at the cats. "So should I avoid traveling while Mercury is in retrograde? You know, like not get on any planes in case they crash?"

Venus chuckled. "Oh, I wouldn't worry. Mercury's only a little planet—the most it can do is delay your flight's departure or arrival. It isn't powerful enough to cause any kind of major accident."

Mercury sighed grumpily at these reassuring words. Without seeming to notice, Venus continued her explanation. "So feel free to travel during retrograde—just make sure to leave yourself plenty of extra time. That doesn't just apply to travel, either—expect the unexpected during this period. As long as you're extra careful, you should be able to avoid running into too much trouble."

"Indeed," Mercury said with a nod. "Just allow for the fact that you're more likely to experience the odd mishap or malfunction."

"Got it," I said.

From now on, I decided I'd check whether the planet was in retrograde and take extra care during those periods, as well as leave early if I had somewhere to be.

"Oh," continued Mercury, "and be very careful if you're signing any major contracts."

"Contracts?"

"Yes. That's important. Mercury is only in retrograde for around three weeks at a time, so you're better off using that time to simply check what the agreement says, and only sealing the deal afterward. If you really can't avoid signing during the retrograde period, then be sure to do so with the utmost care."

"Right," I said with a nod. "Bit of a pain, isn't it, this retrograde thing?"

Mercury looked offended, as if I was blaming him personally.

Venus glanced at her companion, then turned to me. "Actually," she said, shaking her head, "it's not all bad. There's something else you should know about Mercury in retrograde . . ."

●

"Dreams can feel so strangely real."

Megumi's words brought Takashi back to his senses. "Definitely."

Boarding a train and ending up at a pop-up café in the middle of nowhere, drinking a sky-blue cream soda, and being accosted by talking cats . . . strange just about covered it. It was also odd how some parts of the dream had been so hazy, while others were incredibly vivid.

Just like Megumi with her Sunrise Syrup coffee, he could practically still taste the cream soda he'd been served. How had he learned about Mercury in retrograde? He definitely hadn't known a thing about it before. . . .

Now that he thought about it, the cat named Venus had been saying something at the end. What was it again?

There's something else you should know about Mercury in retrograde . . .

He felt sure he'd remember soon, but he couldn't just sit there in silence.

He looked up and met Megumi's gaze. "What about your dream, then? What happened?"

Partly, he just wanted to hear her talk. But he was also dying to know more about the dreams they had both had.

"It's pretty odd, actually," began Megumi, clasping her hands on her lap. "That dream is what persuaded me to quit the salon in Umeda."

"What? You left your job because of . . . a dream?"

She chuckled and nodded. "You bet."

PART TWO:
MOONLIGHT AND VENUS CHAMPAGNE FLOAT

月光と金星のシャンパンフロート

1

"I know, I know—quitting my job because of a dream . . . But I don't regret it one bit."

Takashi nodded, waiting for Megumi to continue.

"See, I've always loved doing my friends' hair or helping people look their best," she began. "So being a hairdresser just felt like my calling, you know? I'd always dreamed of living in a big city, but I didn't quite have the nerve to move to Tokyo, so I settled for the fanciest neighborhood in this part of the country—Umeda. I managed to make it all a reality—and I was so pleased with what I'd achieved."

Her expression darkened. "The thing is, I was doing a job I loved in a place I loved, and yet I couldn't shake the feeling that something wasn't right. You know, a sort of vague discomfort I couldn't quite put my finger on . . ." She sighed. "And then I had this dream . . ."

With a faraway look in her eyes, she began the story of her dream.

●

I was on my way back from work as usual. The only thing that was different was that the salon manager had assembled all the staff to reprimand them, complaining that they weren't bringing in enough customers.

"Except for Megumi, that is, who's as popular as

ever. You could all learn a thing or two from her when it comes to treating the customers right."

The staff in the salon nodded in agreement—including the stylists who'd been there longer than me.

By rights, I should have been over the moon at being praised like this in front of everyone. But instead I felt deflated. I liked being a hairdresser and felt confident in the role—but when it came to my actual skills, I knew I still had a long way to go. I did seem to be popular with customers, but that was mainly because they found me easy or pleasant to interact with. I knew very well that some of my colleagues were much more talented hairdressers.

I was really happy that customers would ask for me in particular—but at the same time, I wasn't filled with a burning desire to become the number one stylist at the salon.

With all these thoughts swimming around in my head, I didn't feel like heading straight home. Instead, I wandered into an izakaya, where I ended up drinking quite a bit more than I'd expected.

After I left the izakaya, things got—peculiar.

I should have been making my way home through Osaka—but for some reason I found myself in the Ote-suji shopping arcade in Kyoto, where my parents' beauty parlor was. Not only that, but it ought to have been the middle of the night by now—and yet it appeared to be early evening, a time of day when the shopping arcade would normally be buzzing with activity. But it was completely deserted.

I wandered down the shopping arcade in a state of total bafflement.

When I reached my parents' beauty parlor, I found a woman standing by the door. She looked vaguely Scandinavian, with wavy platinum-blond hair and blue eyes that seemed tinged with gold. She was quite beautiful.

"Excuse me," she said, looking in my direction. "Is this your beauty parlor?"

"It's my parents', actually. Is everything okay?"

The woman timidly dropped her gaze. "Actually, I have a big show tonight. I was hoping to get my hair and makeup done, but it looks like this place isn't open."

I peered into the beauty parlor, then tried the door. It was locked. Maybe my parents had taken the day off. In any case, they were nowhere to be seen.

"Yeah, they must be closed. I don't have the key, I'm afraid . . ."

What was a woman with film-star looks doing outside my parents' modest old beauty parlor?

Then I felt a jolt of excitement.

"You know, I could do it for you if you like. I work in a salon myself, and I even have my tools with me."

The woman suddenly beamed. "Really? That would be wonderful."

"Of course. The only question is—where?" I glanced around.

"Our café is just this way. Perhaps you could do it there?" With these words, the woman began walking daintily down the street.

"Oh—do you work in the shopping arcade, then?"

"Yes, but just for tonight."

She led me through the gate in the middle of the shopping arcade that led to Daikoji Temple. In the middle of the temple grounds was what looked like a mobile coffee shop, with several sets of tables and chairs positioned in front of a small truck.

She gave a soft chuckle. "We're borrowing this space for the evening, you see."

Just then, a large tortoiseshell cat wearing an apron emerged from the truck and set out a sign. The sign read: THE FULL MOON COFFEE SHOP.

"Master!" my companion called to the cat, raising a hand. "We'll use this table, if you don't mind." A short distance from the truck were several rows of stackable chairs. Sitting in them was a group of foreign-looking men and women. They were clutching musical instruments and chatting among themselves.

I could see a young red-haired man clutching a trumpet; a handsome boy with silver hair and a flute; a plump, kind-looking woman cradling a cello; and a slightly dour-looking man in a black suit gripping a conductor's baton. Most of all, though, my attention was drawn to a strikingly beautiful woman with long, straight hair.

As I gazed in fascination, my blond companion took a seat and turned to me.

"Pretty special, isn't she?"

"Yeah. But then, so are you!"

"Thank you," she said, a smile spreading across her face. "We all work here at the Full Moon Coffee Shop, you see. And sometimes we become the Full Moon Orchestra, too."

At these words, I turned to look at the foreigners clutching their instruments.

"So those are all members of your orchestra?"

"Yes," she said with a nod, "though we're not all here tonight. Just the ones who're connected."

"Connected . . . ?" I tilted my head slightly to one side, not quite knowing what she meant. Even her impeccable Japanese had its limits, it seemed.

"That woman with the black hair is the opera singer. Everyone adores her. I'll be playing the violin at her side this evening."

A slight flush of excitement had come to the woman's cheeks. So that was what she'd meant about having a big show tonight.

"Right," I said, nodding deeply. "Well, I'll make sure you look stunning."

I opened my bag and laid my tools out on the table. I set down a vanity mirror, then fitted the cape around her neck. She seemed to be quivering with a mixture of excitement and nervousness. My own pulse quickened, too—but I wasn't nervous. I knew I had what it took.

I carefully applied makeup to her face, then set

about styling her silken hair. With each touch of my hands, she became even more radiant.

I was so engrossed in my craft that I didn't notice the crimson sky turning a dark blue. When I'd finished, I let out a deep breath.

She inspected herself in the mirror, then beamed at me.

"Thank you for doing such a wonderful job. You're so talented!"

I shook my head. "No, thank *you*. I haven't enjoyed my job this much in a long time . . ."

It was true—for once, I felt completely satisfied. Bringing out the beauty in others really did make me happy.

"Do you mean you don't normally enjoy your work?" asked the woman, a concerned look on her face.

I didn't know how to answer. "Well . . . I do love making people look their best. So in that sense, working in a beauty salon is my dream job. But . . ."

But then why does every day feel so tough?

Unable to finish the sentence, I dropped my gaze.

My companion looked over at the black-haired woman. "You know, she used to be a pop singer. But she stopped enjoying it. She loved singing, and yet she couldn't stop feeling depressed. Then, one day, she gave opera a try. It was a revelation. All this time, she'd really been wanting to sing opera! I wonder if you're in a similar situation to her right now."

Her words echoed deeply within me.

"Thank you, Megumi," she said, bobbing her head in gratitude. Then, with a spring in her step, she made her way over to the orchestra.

How did she know my name?

Soon, however, I had my answer. In the next moment, something happened that told me this could only be a dream.

As soon as my companion took her place alongside the black-haired woman, they both . . . turned into cats.

One was a white-haired Persian. The other was jet black, with striking purple eyes. The two cats shimmered brilliantly, then, as if they'd been swallowed up by the night sky, suddenly vanished from sight.

"What the . . ." I gasped, craning my neck to follow the trail of light that had formed across the sky. Next to the bright full moon, I thought I could see Venus twinkling.

The man in the black suit raised his baton and the orchestra began to play. A beautiful singing voice, accompanied by a violin, seemed to drift down from the sky.

Other customers had taken seats at the other tables by this stage. I could see their outlines, but their faces were obscured—probably because the only source of light was the full moon above.

As I lost myself in the familiar music, the tortoiseshell cat came over, bearing a tray.

"'Nessun Dorma.' From *Turandot*," he said.

Confused, I looked up. The master of the café arched his eyebrows playfully as he set a cocktail glass down on the table.

Inside the glass was a ball of golden ice cream, topped with mint leaves. The cat produced a bottle of champagne, then poured some of it right onto the ice cream.

"A Moonlight and Venus Champagne Float. Try it with some of our luscious strawberries."

He set a small plate of strawberries down by the glass. They appeared to be coated with gold dust.

"How fancy!"

"Tonight's a special night." The master chuckled. "Venus and Full Moon are putting on a concert."

Spoon in hand, I brought a scoop of the golden ice cream to my mouth. The flavor of peach danced across my tongue—sweet, but not overpoweringly so, with the champagne and mint each contributing their own distinct flavors. It was pure elegance—a drink and a dessert all at once.

"This is . . . exquisite!"

The orchestra was still playing, happily focused on their instruments while the black cat's mellifluous voice soared effortlessly over the music.

"She sings so well," I murmured, half to myself. "You know, I hope I find my own version of opera one day . . ."

"Indeed," said the master, before producing a small pocket watch that seemed to have been hanging around his neck. "Mind if I read your stars?"

I found myself agreeing, despite not quite knowing what he meant.

The master pressed the winding crown of the watch inward, then peered at its dials. Suddenly, an enormous horoscope filled the night sky. The master looked up at it, then said, "Ah," as though something had become clear to him. "Venus in your second house."

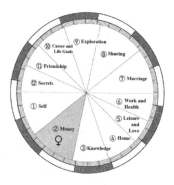

"The second house symbolizes money and possessions. It tells us what kind of method of earning money—a job, in other words—suits us best. Among other things, Venus is the planet of pleasure. So if you want to thrive, the most important thing for you is to find something that you really enjoy."

"Something I enjoy?" I murmured, looking up at the sky.

I thought I *did* enjoy my job. But then why had I been finding it so tough recently? I could think of two reasons. One was that I couldn't work at my own pace: I was constantly dancing to someone else's tune. The other was something that, as a hairdresser, I didn't want to admit.

I didn't actually like cutting hair.

I loved arranging people's hair and doing their makeup, whether it was for coming-of-age ceremonies, weddings, or photo shoots. My confidence lay in making people look their best. But not actually *cutting* hair.

What the master was saying was that I needed to focus on actually doing what I loved.

The mere idea was already making my heart feel lighter.

The dark night sky was brightening. Soon the sun began to rise. Was it really morning already?

"How about an iced coffee to see in the dawn?" The master smiled mischievously as he set a long, narrow glass down in front of me. It was filled with a deep, reddish-purple, almost indigo-colored iced coffee.

Into it he poured a whitish syrup.

"Served with Sunrise Syrup."

The dark color of the iced coffee rapidly brightened. I took a sip through my straw. It was slightly bitter—and at the same time sweet. The flavor sharpened my senses.

Dawn was breaking. I closed my eyes against the dazzling morning light.

●

"And then I woke up and I was lying in bed at home," said Megumi. "Pretty mind-blowing, don't you think?"

Takashi gulped, nodding in shock.

"Sorry. Was that a bit much?" she asked.

He gave a quick shake of his head. "Not at all." Megumi's dream had certainly left him speechless—but only because of how closely it resembled his own.

"Anyway," Megumi continued, "I quit my job at the salon soon afterward."

Takashi looked up. "And decided to help out here instead?"

"Sure, I'm helping them out when I can. But I've actually decided to go freelance."

"Freelance? I didn't know there were freelance stylists."

"Yep. You know, callouts to things like weddings or photo studios. I went into it assuming work would be pretty thin on the ground—at least to start off. But when I gave it a try, I found myself getting all sorts of requests. My parents know someone who does hair for the geisha and maiko in Kyoto, and they said they'd appreciate another pair of hands. And you know that friend who was here a moment ago? Well, she works in TV, and one of the on-set stylists needs an assistant, so she asked if I'd be interested in helping out during busy periods." Megumi's eyes twinkled. "Isn't that great?"

She sighed. "Still, I've been struggling to keep on top of all the messages and bookings that are coming in. I thought it might be a good idea to make my own website."

Sensing that this was his time to shine, Takashi sat up and looked her in the eyes. "Well, let us help you. We'll keep things as affordable as possible—especially if you use one of our templates."

"Really? Thanks!"

"So, what kind of website are you after? I brought some samples, in case that helps." Takashi took a pamphlet from his bag.

"Something simple but sophisticated, so that even individual customers can book me easily if they want to. You know, with a calendar and so on."

"This is just a suggestion, but your hairstyling skills seem pretty amazing. How about featuring a video to showcase them?" Takashi said.

"Yes! I could do something like those three-minute cooking videos, showing people how to easily style their hair."

"No, social media would be your best bet for that kind of thing, but we could link your website to your TikTok."

After a while, Megumi let out an amused chuckle.

"Am I talking too much?" asked Takashi.

"Not at all. Sorry—I'm just impressed. Little Takashi has turned into such a go-getter!" She giggled again.

The last time she'd seen him, he'd been a primary-school kid. Back then, three years was a pretty huge age gap. No wonder she found it strange seeing him all grown up like this.

"You know what?" said Megumi all of a sudden.

"That friend who was just in here getting her hair done—she was in our walk-to-school group, too."

"Seriously? Her, too?"

"And do you remember our teacher, Miss Serikawa? You know, the one who went on to become a screenwriter?"

"Oh—yeah," Takashi said with a nod. Of course he remembered her—they were in fact working together, even if by accident. Now, thinking back, he realized there was a very real reason why Megumi might have remembered him so well.

Megumi looked up at the ceiling, but it was as if she was gazing at something much farther away.

2

Their primary-school days were a distant memory, but one incident was still fresh in both their minds.

Their walk-to-school group had been chaperoned by a substitute teacher named Mizuki Serikawa. Normally, the teachers only accompanied pupils on the way home, but because Miss Serikawa happened to live along the route, she joined them in the mornings, too.

"So, have you all done your homework?" she'd greet them cheerfully in the morning. They were always disappointed when they found out it was her day off.

The incident in question happened on the way home one day, near the play park where they normally all separated. Miss Serikawa was gazing up at an elegant, old Western-style building by the park, a puzzled look on her face.

The house she was looking at belonged to a silver-haired old gentleman who always dressed impeccably. They'd heard he was a pianist who used to perform around the world. He still played, and often on the way home from school they'd hear the sound of the piano drifting from his windows.

When they got to the park, the first- and second-year pupils would be met by their guardians, who would then escort them the rest of the way home. Normally, Miss Serikawa would be all smiles as they exchanged greetings, but that day she was peering transfixed at the old man's house.

"What's wrong, Miss?" asked one of the older

pupils. Seeming to come back to her senses, Miss Serikawa looked down at him. Her expression was troubled.

"Unless it's raining, that old gentleman always has his windows open in the morning, no matter how cold it gets. And in the early evening he plays the piano, and if he's not doing that he's always gardening. But his windows have been closed since yesterday, even though it's been sunny. And we haven't heard the piano or seen him in the garden . . ."

The pupils exchanged confused looks.

"Did he really have the windows open every day?" asked one.

"Do you think he's gone on vacation?" asked another.

Miss Serikawa gave a strained chuckle. "You know, he adopted a bunch of abandoned cats recently. He was just telling me the other day how he couldn't go on vacation with them running around the house. This is a little worrying . . . I'll just try ringing the intercom."

She walked over to the house. The remaining pupils in the group filed along behind her.

Takashi had been one of those pupils. He didn't

remember this part, but it seemed both Akari—the group leader—and Megumi had been there, too.

Miss Serikawa took a deep breath, then buzzed the intercom. There was no reply. Instead, a large number of cats appeared at the window, mewing desperately for help.

"Looks like something really is wrong."

Miss Serikawa immediately rang the police, who came to check the house. It turned out the old gentleman had spent the last few days in bed, unable to move because he was so ill.

An ambulance arrived soon afterward, and the old man was carried out on a stretcher. The cats wanted to follow him. No matter how much they were chased away, they kept jumping onto his stretcher. The old man looked on weakly from where he lay.

"How about we look after them for you until you're better?" asked Miss Serikawa.

The old man looked immensely relieved. "Thank you," he said, handing over his keys.

The guardians who'd been waiting in the park muttered among themselves. "Taking someone's keys like that—there's no telling what sort of trouble that might lead to," said one of them dubiously.

"It's only until he gets back," replied Miss Serikawa with a smile.

And so Miss Serikawa and her walk-to-school group began looking after the cats every day: feeding them in the morning, feeding them in the evening, and cleaning up their mess.

"Don't worry, you lot," Miss Serikawa would say to the cats as she and the children saw to their various needs. "I'm sure he'll be home before too long."

But the old gentleman never made it home. Around a month after he'd been taken to the hospital, he took his last breath within its walls. The cats had been jumping up on his stretcher because they knew, somehow, that it would be the last time they saw him. And they wanted to say goodbye.

After he passed away, they found out more about him. He'd originally been the conductor of a foreign orchestra. One day, he'd abruptly decided to be a pianist instead. Having devoted his entire life to music, he'd never married. With no children of his own, he'd looked after his adopted cats as if they were his family. There was a nephew who was going to inherit his entire estate, though they'd never been particularly close.

The nephew announced that he was going to sell the house and take the cats to an animal shelter. Worried the cats might be put to sleep, Miss Serikawa and her pupils tried desperately to negotiate with him.

"Give us just a bit more time. We'll definitely find them foster homes!"

But the nephew insisted he wanted to sell the house as soon as possible and the cats were an issue.

The pupils were bitter about the situation. They all wanted to help the cats if they could. But no one was in a position to give them a home.

Takashi ran home to ask his parents: *What if they looked after the cats at his house?*

His family ran a construction business, and they had a shed for storing all their materials. Another cat had taken up residence there in the past, and had seemed very comfortable. With this argument, Takashi managed to win his family over. His kind-hearted parents said the cats could stay in the shed until they found foster homes, as long as the children looked after them properly.

And so the cats began living in the shed, and Miss Serikawa and her pupils looked after them every day.

Not long afterward, all their efforts paid off. Foster homes were found, and the cats set off for their new families.

•   •   •

"I remember it so well!" said Megumi. "That moment when it looked like they'd have to go to an animal shelter, and you came dashing over to the park and said, 'We can look after them at my house!' I was so happy I almost cried!"

Even now, as she remembered the episode, tears filled her eyes. She propped her head in her hands. Not quite knowing what to do, Takashi looked down at the floor.

It was all coming back to him, too. When he'd said they could look after the cats at his place, one of the older pupils had turned to him, tears streaming down her face, and said, "Thank you!"

Megumi had said she'd almost cried, but as he remembered it, she'd been crying her eyes out. The sight of her sobbing away like that was something he'd never forget. There was no doubt about it: that had been Megumi.

"Maybe it was their way of saying thanks."

Megumi blinked. "Sorry?"

"You know, that dream of yours. With the cats. Maybe they were repaying the favor somehow."

She smiled slightly. "We all looked after them together, didn't we? I don't see why they would have rewarded me in particular. Plus, none of the old man's cats looked anything like that beautiful Persian or the black one with purple eyes."

This was true, thought Takashi. The cats they'd looked after had all been ordinary short-haired types. "Well, then," he blurted, "maybe the cats asked the cat god to repay the favor on their behalf."

Megumi burst out laughing. "The *cat god*? Now there's something I never thought I'd hear you say . . ."

Takashi felt his cheeks redden. She was right—that definitely wasn't the kind of thing he usually came out with.

"And if the cats *did* ask the cat god to repay the favor," Megumi went on, "shouldn't you be the one getting the reward?"

"Me?"

"I mean, you're the one who saved them, right? The rest of us were just fretting."

"But that was only because I happened to have somewhere I could look after them!"

It was then that Takashi remembered the end of his dream.

Actually, it's not all bad. There's something else you should know about Mercury in retrograde...

It's a time for looking back on the past. Not everything has to move forward all the time, you know...

Retrograde is when you take another look at your life. It's when you bump into old acquaintances, and get another shot at things that didn't work out the first time around...

That was it, thought Takashi, smiling to himself. When he'd seen that older girl with the tear-stricken face, something inside him had soared.

The gap between a third-year student and a sixth-year one was enormous—and yet he'd felt a strange, almost painful urge to protect her. He hadn't realized it at the time, but it was the moment he first fell in love. Now that same feeling, a mixture of pleasure and pain, was welling up inside him again. It had been almost two decades since then. A bizarre series of events had brought his first love back into his life, and now here she was, sitting at his side. For a moment, he hadn't even recognized her. But that was only on the surface. Deep down, it seemed, he remembered her perfectly.

That was why he'd felt so drawn to her from the moment they bumped into each other—and so nervous about this meeting that he'd been unable to sleep.

It's when you get another shot at things that didn't work out the first time around. By teaching him about the stars, the Persian cat had given him the push he needed.

"You know, I think they might have rewarded me, too," murmured Takashi.

"Really? How'd you mean?"

"Well, I might just be imagining it . . ." he replied, scratching his head.

"Go on," said Megumi, her eyes gleaming as she leaned forward to listen. "Tell me everything."

There were all kinds of things he wanted to tell her. But, he decided, there was one thing he'd save until the retrograde was over—turning to her with the words: *You know, I think I was in love with you.*

Yes, that part could come later.

For now, he simply looked her in the eyes—and smiled gently.

EPILOGUE

1

Mizuki Serikawa took one look at the email from the company that made the dating game, clenched her fists, and exclaimed, "Yes!"

On the phone screen in front of her were the following words: "We're introducing a new main character—and we'd like you to write him."

Mizuki had poured her heart and soul into writing the ending of the side character. But the results had surpassed even her expectations. Her character had gone viral, and she'd even been asked to do an interview. If she was going to reveal her identity, she decided, now was the time. And so she'd announced to the world that she was in fact the once-famous Mizuki Serikawa.

She'd been expecting a mixed response at best. In the end, though, it had been overwhelmingly positive. Now all she had to do was focus on writing the script for the main character. If she pulled that off, who knew where it might lead?

"Right, then," she said, firing herself up as she began brewing some tea.

She was living in the same cheap studio apartment as before. But ever since her night at that mysterious coffee shop, she'd decided that, however small her place was, she'd make it into somewhere she actually wanted to live. With that in mind, she'd embarked on a modest renovation.

When she wasn't using her bed, she'd make it up neatly and cover it with cushions so that it became a sofa. She'd placed a decorative plant next to her small dining table, together with a floor lamp. If you only looked at that corner of the room, she thought to herself with satisfaction, you'd think you were in a café. She'd also started putting out flowers—even just one made all the difference.

She couldn't afford new curtains, but she'd replaced the tassels that held them in place with fancier ones. She stopped using the mugs she'd bought as a stopgap measure from a hundred-yen shop and replaced them with ones she actually liked.

At home, she decided, everything she set her eyes on should bring her joy. Just making that little effort every day was enough to gradually brighten her spirits.

It was just as that star-reading cat, the master of the café, had explained: having a pleasant home was vital to her happiness.

She got out the elegant cup and saucer she'd splashed out on, poured her tea, and sat down at the table.

Glancing out of the window, she noticed that tortoiseshell cat sitting on her balcony railing again. It looked at her and mewed loudly.

"*What are you trying to tell me...?*"

In an instant, she remembered the elderly gentleman who had been drinking his coffee in that strange dream. He'd been trying to tell her something, too. What had it been? He'd spoken too quietly for her to hear, so perhaps there was no use wondering what it was.

Right, she thought, trying to focus, as she opened up her computer and took a sip of her tea. *Time to check my emails...*

Since that star-reading session in her dream, she'd begun to take an interest in astrology and had even done a bit of reading on the subject.

Ah, Mercury's in retrograde. Better watch out!

Second chances, huh... Maybe it's time to send Akari another pitch.

She planned to transform her previous pitch into something more suitable for the Age of Aquarius. If she could just convey that to Akari ...

Checking her inbox, she saw an email from Akari herself. Her heart almost flew out of her chest. Barely able to contain her excitement, she opened the email.

Sorry we couldn't talk longer the other day, especially after you had made time for me. Unfortunately, the executives decided your pitch wasn't quite in tune with the times, but I actually think it was pretty decent. Do you think you could rework it slightly and come up with something that feels a bit more "current"?

Mizuki gulped. It looked as if it really was the time for second chances.

Let's do this.

She stared fiercely at the keyboard in front of her, then typed the words: "Thank you."

Just then, the face of that gentleman from her dream flashed back into her mind. All of a sudden, she could hear his voice again, more clearly this time.

Thank you.

Yes, that was it. He had been thanking her.

2

Akari Nakayama was sitting at the counter of a bistro bar, gazing out at the Kamo River—and waiting for Jiro.

On the other side of the counter was a large window. The sun had long since set and a beautiful full moon hung in the sky.

Another full moon...

Reaching for her phone, she glimpsed her reflection in its dark screen. She'd had her hair done by her friend Megumi, and the result was so stunning that she almost felt self-conscious. Well, she thought, at least it would convince Jiro of Megumi's talents. Nodding to herself, she checked the news on her phone.

Satsuki Ayukawa, the actress, was trending.

After that peculiar evening in the park, Satsuki had decided to hold a press conference. Without blaming the man involved in the slightest, she'd apologized to his wife and children—and the many fans who'd been upset by the news. Of course, no matter how much she apologized, there were plenty of people who refused to forgive her. But then, on the evening of the same day, the actor who'd cheated on his wife with her had held a press conference of his own—in which he completely denied any responsibility for what had happened.

"It's just like she said—she's entirely to blame for all this. I wasn't at fault."

And with that, the brunt of the public's anger shifted from Satsuki to him. Not only that, but the actor was found to have been involved with *another* woman at the time when Satsuki was his mistress.

Satsuki began to be seen as the victim—someone who'd had the misfortune to get involved with a worthless wretch of a man. Now, slowly but surely, she was becoming a regular fixture on television once more.

An online article reported what she'd said on a TV show: "I think I'm done with romance for the time being."

Sure, there were a few of the usual derogatory comments. But these were outnumbered by others like: "That's right—men only let you down. Focus on the acting!" and "Watch out for trash like him in the future!"

The mere sight of her holding her head high like that, whatever people said, had given Akari courage, too.

As she waited, she checked her email and found a reply from Mizuki Serikawa.

Thank you. I'd love to. I'll give it my best shot!

Akari couldn't help but smile.

"Ooh!" came a voice from her side. "Someone's looking gorgeous tonight!"

She looked up to find Jiro. He was sporting a casual T-shirt and jeans.

"Oh, hi!"

"Sorry to keep you waiting," he said, taking a seat at her side. They each ordered a craft beer, then clinked their glasses together.

"That friend I was telling you about did my hair."

"Oh, you mean the freelancer you said might be able to lend a hand?"

"That's the one. She said she'd love to work with you."

"The pleasure would be all mine. Just look at that braiding! Really suits you, too. I can tell she knows what she's doing!"

"Thanks," said Akari nervously.

"You know, you're looking better than ever these days. Got yourself a boyfriend or something? Let me guess: that was a message from him you were smiling about just now."

Akari almost choked on her drink. "No boyfriend. It was an email from Mizuki."

"You mean the Mizuki whose script you told me you rejected?"

"Yep," Akari said with a nod. "After that, I couldn't stop thinking about what you said . . ."

"Oh, dear." Jiro put a hand to his cheek. "What did I say?"

" 'When you put yourself out there like that and get a straight-up rejection, it can really floor you. Unless you're naturally confident, sticking to your guns is *hard*.' "

"Did I really say that?"

"And that I was tough on both myself and others."

"I do remember that part."

"But I've been thinking it might be a good idea to cut down on that—even if just a little at first. You know, spoil myself sometimes. Maybe 'spoil' isn't the right word. I mean, just listen to what I really want and accept it. If I could manage to do that, even just a little . . ."

Jiro chuckled in response.

"What, did I say something funny?"

"It was that 'just a little' at the end. I guess you're not one to change *too* quickly, are you?"

Akari smiled ruefully. "I guess not."

"But it's definitely important to learn to indulge

yourself, even if it's only little by little. I learned that the hard way!"

"How do you mean?" Akari glanced sideways at Jiro.

"See, I grew up in a strict household. My parents are both pretty hardheaded. Kept telling me I had to become a civil servant. And I gave it a decent shot, too. But somewhere along the way, I just started to feel really . . . stifled. Like I couldn't breathe. Then one day, acting on impulse, I tried on my older sister's dress. I wanted the thrill of doing something naughty. And my dad walked in on me."

"Damn. What happened?" asked Akari, leaning forward slightly, her heart beating faster.

"He really laid into me. Called me a pervert and a disgrace. So then I flipped, too. *That's right, Dad! I shouted. This is the real me, okay, and it always has been!* Then he whacked me as hard as he could, and disowned me on the spot." Jiro chuckled.

"What did you do after that?"

"I stayed at my grandmother's on my mom's side until I finished high school. After that I started work-ing at a beauty salon, got my qualifications, one thing led to another, and now I'm here. So there you have it—the story of my dramatic transformation."

"Jiro, that must have been so tough."

"I hurt my parents, and our family basically fell apart. But if things had stayed the way they were, I'd have been the one to break. A change like that was the only way for me to get a handle on my own life." After another short laugh, Jiro rested his cheek on his hand and shrugged. "Still, I do feel bad about my parents. We've patched things up slightly since then, but I've never been back to the family home."

"But if they'd properly understood what you were going through and taken your feelings into account, things would never have escalated like that. I don't think you need to blame yourself . . ."

As they chatted, there was one thing Akari was desperate to find out: where, exactly, Jiro's romantic interests lay.

She decided to take the plunge. "Can I ask you something?"

"Sure, what?" said Jiro, blinking.

"You know how, well, you have a certain way of talking . . . Is that how you feel inside, too?"

"How I feel inside?"

"What I mean is . . . Well, I was wondering whether you were more into men or women . . ."

The words had suddenly rolled off her tongue. She trailed off as she began to regret saying anything at all.

Jiro gave Akari a sidelong glance. "Oh, dear. I wonder what you're hoping I'll say?"

Akari felt her pulse quicken. "Well, I guess that if you told me you were into . . . women, that would be . . . nice."

"Why's that?" asked Jiro, his expression blank.

"Well, it's just . . ."

"Because otherwise I might want to chat about guy-on-guy manga with you or something?"

"No, not at all . . . I was just . . ."

"Curious?" Jiro grinned.

Akari was at a loss for words. Jiro was sharp. He'd probably already worked out what she was getting at and was just toying with her. Akari clenched her fists and decided to squeeze the words out.

"Well, it's because I like you."

Jiro froze.

His eyes had opened wide. "What, seriously?"

Unable to find the words, Akari simply nodded.

"But . . . I was so sure someone like you would never be interested in me. As a man, I mean."

It seemed that, however sharp his intuition, Jiro had been completely in the dark about her feelings.

Akari had made her decision. She'd learned to trust her heart. She'd accepted her feelings for what they were. That was the important thing, she reminded herself.

"Anyway," she continued in a quiet voice, "maybe I'm not what you're after, but I just wanted you to know that I like you. I really do."

Jiro remained silent.

What was wrong? Akari turned fearfully to look— and found him blushing a bright red.

"Jiro . . . ?"

"Hang on, Akari," he said, covering his face with his hands. "This is against the rules . . ."

Akari stared at him in surprise.

"I mean, look at me," he murmured. "I'm all in a flutter! See, the thing is, it *is* women I'm into . . ."

Now it was Akari's turn to feel her face burning.

Outside, someone was playing the piano. The notes drifting on the wind sounded like a blessing.

3

On the banks of the swiftly flowing Kamo River, the Full Moon Coffee Shop had appeared once again. The gentle sound of the piano filled the air.

The cats that staffed the café had shut up shop for the day and were sitting in the outdoor chairs, their eyes squinting as they let the music wash over them. By the river stood a jet-black grand piano. Seated at it was an elderly gentleman, the light of the full moon illuminating him like a spotlight. He was playing Elgar's *Salut d'Amour.*

When he finished, the cats applauded enthusiastically and hurried over to him. The gentleman got to his feet, stroked the cats on their heads and chins, then made his way toward the café.

The master set down a glass of beer for him on one of the freshly wiped tables. "Here you are. A Celestial Beer."

The liquid in the glass was a gradation of different colors, from dark blue and indigo to sky blue and orange. Even more striking were the countless tiny stars that seemed to speckle the beer, including what looked like the Milky Way.

The gentleman's features creased into a smile as he took his seat. "Sorry—I know you've already closed for the night."

"Not at all," said the master, putting a paw to his chest. "Consider it a thank-you for that magnificent performance."

"Actually, that was supposed to be my way of thanking all of *you.*"

"Thanking us?"

"For showing those kids the way forward in life." The old man got to his feet and gave a deep bow. "I really am grateful."

"Oh, you don't need to thank us. They helped our

friends out of a tight spot once—if anything, we owe *them.*" The master smiled, then glanced at the seat opposite the old man. "Mind if I join you?"

"Please."

The two sat down opposite each other. Another Celestial Beer was brought out for the master, and the two of them clinked their glasses together. The gentleman took a sip of the beer, then closed his eyes and nodded.

"That's really something. I can almost feel it spreading through me."

"Glad you like it."

"Brings back memories, too. The first drink I ever had at this place was a beer, too."

"Was it?"

"Yes," said the gentleman with a gentle smile. "Remember, on that street corner in Prague? You served me a beer and told me to relax my shoulders. I'll never forget how good that beer tasted."

"Ah, yes. You were still a young conductor back then—in your Mars phase, if I remember correctly."

"I never quite knew what you meant by 'young,' when I was already in my forties. But now, looking back, I can see I was still a mere stripling, really—and arrogant to boot. The more famous I got, the more demanding I became—sometimes to the point of being overbearing. I began seeing the members of my orchestra as mere conduits for my music . . ."

Yet all he'd wanted was to make the most magnificent music he could . . . Tormented by worry, he'd been on the verge of falling out of love with music itself.

Then, one day, walking the banks of the Vltava, he'd spotted a mysterious-looking mobile café by the Charles Bridge. And it was there that he'd met the large tortoiseshell cat for the first time.

"You have Pluto in your first house," the cat had told him. "It's a very powerful planet, you know. Having it in your first house, which governs the self, suggests you have plenty of charisma, but also a tendency to obsess over details; you can be relentless in the pursuit of perfection. When that side of you shows itself, it can be hard for those around you to keep up."

He'd found it hard not to agree. The urge to create his own music was something he'd never be able to let go of. And no matter how much soul-searching this advice triggered, he knew that once he stood in front of the orchestra, he'd carry on making impossible demands—all in the name of turning the music in his head into a reality.

"Well, how about going solo for a change?"

"Going . . . solo?"

"Yes. For example, on that instrument over there."

He'd looked in the direction the master was pointing, seen the grand piano, and fallen silent. Before becoming a conductor, he'd been an accomplished musician—of course, he knew his way around the piano. And there was a reason why people said it was an orchestra all by itself. For a single instrument, the range of music it could express was enormous.

Right. Before I start bossing people about with my baton, maybe I should master my own music.

He got up and walked over to the piano.

"I wish you luck," said the master from behind him. "Pluto is the planet of destruction, but also of rebirth. As one of your fans, I'll be looking forward to your grand comeback."

He'd turned around, but by then the mysterious café had disappeared.

● ● ●

"After that, I decided I'd focus on creating music on the piano. If I could manage that to my satisfaction, maybe then I'd be able to return to conducting." He sighed. "The thing is, I was never quite satisfied. And so I realized something."

The master gave him a puzzled look. "What was that?"

"If I couldn't express the music properly myself, then I couldn't very well go about ordering the orchestra to 'play it with more feeling,' could I? In the end, I became so obsessed with the piano that I never went back to conducting."

"Indeed," said the master with a nod. "And you became world famous as a pianist instead."

"Sounds rather impressive, doesn't it? But before I knew it, I was an aging bachelor with nothing but music to fill my days. In my old age, I remodeled the house I'd inherited from my parents and lived out my days playing the piano there."

The gentleman propped his chin on his hand.

Having being "saved" by a cat himself, the sight

of those abandoned kittens had been impossible to ignore. He'd taken them home without a moment's hesitation. In the end, though, they had been the ones to save him.

"Those kids were my saviors, too. Greeting me so cheerfully in the mornings and evenings, listening to my playing with delighted looks on their faces . . . Oh, how I used to look forward to them coming past in the evening! I'd get all excited thinking about what I'd play for them this time . . . And they carried on being my saviors right to the end."

"And you wanted to do them a favor in return?" asked the master.

The gentleman nodded gently. "In each of those kids, I felt as if I could see myself as a young man. I spent all those years conducting, obsessing over the perfect performance, when all I really wanted was to sit at the piano and play. It was the same with love. In my youth I fell in love with a divorced woman many years older than me. But people told me she wasn't right for me, and so I suppressed my feelings for her entirely. Before I knew it, she was engaged to another man. I burned with regret, blaming myself for being too proud to make the right decision. . . . Even now, I still wonder what could have been if I'd only been more honest with myself. I was determined to teach those kids never to shy away from being themselves.

"Besides, this is a turbulent time. One era is ending, a new one beginning. There may be many hardships and challenges to come, but knowing the stars makes life a lot easier. That's what I wanted them to know. And you, Master, were the one who taught me that in the first place."

"I suppose I was," replied the master nostalgically, his eyes becoming crescent moons as he smiled. "Your natal chart is a record of your destiny, the compass of your existence. To make your own way in life, first you need to know yourself. As star readers, that's something we want as many people as possible to learn."

The master and the gentleman gazed at each other for a moment. Then the gentleman finished his beer and got to his feet.

"Right, then. One last piece. Beethoven's *Pathétique*.

"Isn't that quite a sad one?"

"Not at all. Mizuki heard me playing it here the other day, you know. I think she grasped what I was trying to get across. I was over the moon."

By the time Beethoven wrote the *Pathétique*, he was already suffering from serious hearing loss—and when you listened to it with that in mind, it certainly sounded rather sorrowful. But, thought the gentleman, that melancholy exterior concealed hidden reserves of warmth and strength. It was as though Beethoven was willing us to accept our circumstances and move forward in life. From rock bottom to rebirth: it was basically Pluto in musical form, a melody to comfort and support anyone going through tough times.

Music for a wounded heart.

Remembering Mizuki's words, he seated himself at the piano.

Above, the moon was large and shimmering. For just a moment, it almost seemed to smile.

The gentleman sighed—and began to play.

ACKNOWLEDGMENTS

Not long after I had the idea of writing a book about astrology, I came across a series of illustrations depicting a mysterious Full Moon Coffee Shop run by a cat. I fell in love with them at first sight. The beautiful, dreamlike world of the Full Moon Coffee Shop seemed to go on forever, just like the night sky. Without these illustrations, and the artist behind them, Chihiro Sakurada, this story would never have been born. I would like to take this opportunity to express my deep gratitude.

—Mai Mochizuki

ABOUT THE AUTHOR

Mai Mochizuki is the author of *The Full Moon Coffee Shop* and winner of the Everystar Ebook Grand Prix. She is a member of Mystery Writers of Japan and the Unconventional Mystery Writers Club.

ABOUT THE TYPE

This book was set in Walbaum, a typeface designed in 1810 by German punch cutter J. E. (Justus Erich) Walbaum (1768–1839). Walbaum's type is more French than German in appearance. Like Bodoni, it is a classical typeface, yet its openness and slight irregularities give it a human, romantic quality.